THE CAPE

OVERDRIVE

A DARK SPORES NOVEL

THE CAPE

OVERDRIVE

A DARK SPORES NOVEL

BRAXTON A. COSBY

Cosby Media Productions
Inspiring the Mind and Touching the Soul

Cosby Media Productions ™
Innovation the Mind and Inspiring the Soul

ISBN-13: 978-1983784958
ISBN-10: 1983784958

TABLE OF CONTENTS

ACT I

"The only true way to clearly determine the difference between a hero and a villain is to delineate the motivation behind the actions of each. The desire, no matter how skewed or appropriate, hinges on the intent to protect and preserve the well-being of the multitudes, not the individual."

A. G. Corvington, 48th President of the United States, during his latest State of The Union address concerning the rise of Super-Normals

Chapter 1
Mythos

"All right, I've got four perps heading in the back door," Paladin said as he slowed to a stop across the rooftop of an abandoned warehouse building, one of many filling the landscape of the docks. "Move it," he whispered. His eyes darted from the alleyway to the front door of the adjacent structure—a shipyard that housed over a dozen of Chicago's finest ships—in hopes that Blurr would appear. He gently tapped the side of his helmet as if to bring the comm back to life and force some resemblance of her voice against the sickening quiet of the night. But he heard nothing.

"Come on, Karla," he pleaded, his voice rising. When she failed to respond again, he jumped to the ledge and scanned the alley once more. The first set of four goons were gone while another set of six to eight—armed to the teeth with a shiny assortment of assault rifles, choppers, and handguns—quickly slithered from the alley and into the back entrance of the shipping yard. Paladin reached into the backpack slung over his shoulder, retrieved the strength breastplate, and quickly slapped it into the module on his chest in one smooth motion. The S3 suit expanded around his body as the black armor plating along his frame stiffened across his torso and appendages, filling the gaps between them.

"Going in, Lydia," he said, balancing himself along the ledge. Just as he was about to leap, a strong hand snatched him by the arm.

"Have faith," Zenith said in a smooth, calm tone.

Paladin's head snapped in his direction. "Zenith? What are you doing here?"

"Watching… as usual."

"I thought you didn't want to get caught in the meddlesome affair of *Normals*," Paladin said in a sarcastic tone, particularly enunciating the word "Normals" in a dry pitch.

Zenith's eyes glowed a luminous white that was bright enough to paint the entire black Chicago skyline. "Who said I was getting caught up," his voice boomed.

Paladin took a half-step back, careful not to piss off arguably the most powerful and cryptic of all Super-Normals. Although categorizing him in such a way seemed excessive, it was all scientists could do until further research proved him to be otherwise. From what anyone knew of Zenith, inconclusive sightings of a being floating around the city predated the arrival of the Storm that created Super-Normals—both good and bad—thus, supporting the conjecture that he was a foreigner to the planet earth altogether.

Paladin couldn't pass one bit of judgment, knowing full well that he, too, wasn't spawned from the Dark Spore-laced petri-dish experiment that fateful night, electing to use his vast wealth to construct a super suit to help solve the mysterious Normal murder and restore peace to the city of Chicago.

Paladin held up a hand. "Hey, we're on the same team, pal."

"There's no '*I*' in team," Zenith said.

Paladin could make out the slightest crease along the corner of Zenith's lips. "Is that a *smile* I see breaking across your face, Zenith?" he asked while pointing a finger at Zenith.

"No, it's a smirk," Zenith replied. "And that was a two-fold observation. There is no '*I*' in the word 'team,' and *I* am on nobody's team."

Paladin turned his attention fully to Zenith. "You're going to have to choose one day, Z. You know that, right?"

Zenith did not reply; he only turned his eyes back toward the shipyard. "There she is."

Paladin followed his gaze. "Where? I don't see her."

"Give it a few seconds…three, two, one…now."

Just then, the front door to the shipyard exploded, and Blurr rocketed through the cloud of dark smoke. Bullets whizzed through the air as the sound of machine-gun fire filled the air. Twelve men emptied from the building in pursuit, trying to get a bead on the baby blue and gold streak of light weaving between the bullets.

Blurr came to a halt and wagged a finger at a group of them, taunting, "Aww, you can do better than that boys, can't you?"

The men formed a makeshift half-circle in front of her and as if on cue, sent volleys of bullets her way. As the munitions rained upon her, Blurr held her ground, dodging every shot with ease by merely rocking her body from side to side in all directions.

"It's like there's ten of her," one of the men shouted, noting the ghost images left behind in her wake of lost time.

"Fire at all of 'em then," another shouted.

Countless numbers of bullets whizzed in Blurr's direction, but not one was a match for her shifty moves. She easily dodged each one, emptying the clips of each one of the men's weapons. The sound of hammer clicks replaced the boom of gunfire until the last bullet futilely released from its barrel.

Blurr plucked the bullet from the air with her fingertips and blew a kiss at it before hurling it back at the main leader of the group. The bullet plunged into his shoulder at a speed some ten times faster than its original burst, sending him flying backward through the crowd. "Anyone else?" she asked with a wry smile.

The goons threw their guns down and scurried to take out smaller handguns strapped to their legs and torsos. Before they could manage to get off another salvo of fire, Paladin dropped from the sky and landed between them and Blurr. The ground shattered beneath his feet, sending ripples of cracks around him and making a few of the men lose their footing and topple over. Paladin rose and held up an open hand. "I'd quit while I'm ahead if I were you guys. Turn yourselves in now while you still can. One bloodied body is enough, don't you think," he pleaded.

Paladin peeked over at Blurr, hopeful that the men would take him up on his offer before she lost patience. Ever since he'd assisted her on her Mob Boss hunting crusade over a week ago, she'd grown more relentless with laying a heavy hand of whip-ass on countless enemies,

4

killing a few and mortally wounding hundreds of others. He blindly followed her lead on this, only questioning her once about what she was truly looking for. She blew him off, feeding him some garbage about "a hunch" and asking him to just trust her. And how could he deny her seeing as though she had equally trusted him some time ago when he was only known to her as the infamous hero-to-be Paladin, not the old, geeky high school friend named Sebastian?

But that was a different time entirely. She was the wayward vixen running around with Dark Phase while he was in the middle of trying to solve a murder mystery. And when it all ballooned into a climactic battle with Caine, followed by an unexpected departure of Thief to who knows where, the only thing they both had left was each other— which wasn't a bad thing at all in Sebastian's mind. He'd finally been reunited with the girl of his dreams and, if all he had to do was deal with a little emotional collateral damage here and there to keep her, he'd readily do so.

The sound of a stray explosion against his helmet snapped him back to reality. No sooner than he identified the assailant to his right, Blurr had pounced on him, effectively separating his arm from his hand and slamming what remained against a garbage dumpster. As she ran past Paladin, she cried, "Speed burst!"

"No," Paladin screamed. But it was too late. He had just enough time to catch the hand before it could hit the ground, still clutching the pistol. Blurr's display immediately alerted him to the proximity of a pair of E.I.Es hovering overhead to take in the brawl.

Seconds later, Blurr plowed into the remaining goons, dropping them to the ground one after another and singlehandedly tying their hands behind their backs while linking them together like carts of a train. When she was done, she came to a halt next to Paladin and patted the dust from her hands. She rested her fists on her hips and observed her handy work with a proud smile. "Nice."

"Hmm, hmm," Paladin grunted. "Where'd you find the rope?"

Blurr tilted her head in the opposite direction. "It was about two blocks down Plymouth behind that old junkyard. I noticed it on the way in. It's funny, the thought of using it tonight tickled my brain, but I blew it off as a silly idea. Woman's intuition, huh?"

"Bad…ass," Lydia yelled over the comms. "Nice job, Blurr."

Blurr took a bow and tapped her earpiece comm. "Thank you, *cousin*." When she straightened, she staggered a bit and touched her forehead, eyes shut tight.

"You okay?" Paladin asked.

Blurr waved him off. "I'm fine. Just got a little dizzy, that's all."

"All that churning and burning. Badass!" Lydia said.

Paladin walked over to the men, knelt, and checked their wrists. "Don't encourage her," he said, somewhat annoyed.

"What gives?" Blurr asked.

Paladin stood. "Nothing," he said, deciding to forgo any arguments. "I just wanted to make sure you didn't tighten the ropes too hard."

"Why do you care, anyway?" Blurr asked. "They're nothing but slime balls, slinging drugs and weapons throughout the city as if it's okay. A couple of rope burns is a slap on the wrist if you ask me."

"Slap on the wrist… great wordplay, *cousin*," Lydia said.

"Really, Lydia," Paladin interjected.

The sound of sirens bled into the conversation, and Paladin turned away from the men to swap out his strength breastplate for the speed one he'd just wrenched from his backpack. As his suit shrunk to about half its previous size, slowly contracting around his frame, Zenith appeared before him, eyeing his chest.

"Se–Crets," Zenith whispered, gazing intently.

"As if you didn't already know, I wasn't really a Normal. No *secrets* ever miss you, Zenith." The suit completed its transformation, and Paladin slid the strength breastplate back into his bag. "I saw the new promo add for Perfect Safe security systems, by the way. Big pay-off for you, huh?"

"It was lucrative," Zenith replied.

"What do you do with all that cash anyway?" Blurr asked, leaning in over Paladin's shoulder.

Zenith began to float away. "What everyone else does, speedster. I spend it."

As the sound of cop cars closed in, Zenith vanished and Blurr rested her chin on Paladin's shoulder as her hands slid in from behind and clasped in front on his stomach. "Ready to go, babe?"

Paladin melted, as usual. "Yeah, let's go home."

She kissed the side of his helmet where his cheek would be, and the two of them raced alongside each other, building at full speed. They went on like this, clearing a few more buildings until they finally landed along the top of a taller high-rise to take a break.

Blurr was barely winded, but Paladin always felt the effects from torqueing out at full speed; unlike Blurr, whose talents we supernaturally infused into her DNA, his were derived from the adaptations of his super suit. His lungs and heart always told him when to take a break. Blurr had almost developed a sixth sense of his fatigue and knew just when to pump the brakes a bit. She perched along the edge of the building just a few feet away from Paladin, who stared across the midnight sky. The view of Chicago from this height was breathtaking, but nothing like the sweet silhouette of the woman before him, clad in tight-fitting baby blue and gold apparel. Her hair swirled around her face from the Chicago breeze as she watched him from the corner of her eye.

Paladin took off his helmet and went alongside her. He wrapped his arms around her and gave a firm squeeze. "You're worth all the trouble you are, you know that?" he asked.

"What trouble?" she whispered.

"The good kind."

She turned to him, still fastened in his grasp. "Well, I want to give you some more *trouble* tonight if you're up to it."

He smiled as the blood burned in his cheeks. "When haven't I been?"

Blurr planted a kiss on his lips that seared him from the inside out. He pulled back. "Wait a minute. You did it again, Karla."

"Did what, baby?" she asked in a sultry tone.

He sighed. "You killed those men back there and you know I always lecture you on keeping your cool right after, but instead, this time, you used your beauty to distract me…*again*."

She pushed away. "Well, as I recall, you didn't seem to be too mad about being *distracted* last time."

"Come on, Karla. You know I'm only saying something to you about it because I care about you. I don't want you to get too comfortable killing people, no matter how deserving they may be."

"I know," she said. "I just—sometimes I can't control myself. It all happens so fast. I just want to do so much, but I don't have time to do it right."

Sebastian took her by the arms. "You don't have to do it all by yourself, Karla. That's why I'm here."

"I know. I'm just so used to being a lone wolf."

"Not anymore. You have me, and I'm not ever leaving your side."

"Promise?"

Sebastian tightened his grip on her arms. "Always." He kissed her again, and when he finished, he continued his lecture. "What happened back there, anyway? The dizzy spells?"

"It was nothing. At least, I think it's nothing. I've been getting them from time to time when I use my speed. Lydia said it's probably just the space-time continuum playing tricks on my mind."

"Lydia? You told her about it and not me?" Sebastian asked.

Karla fixed her lips into a smile and began to purr. "You're so cute when you're concerned for me."

Sebastian shook his head. "Focus, Karla. Beyond the killing, you were reckless back there. Barging through that shipyard all by yourself. That wasn't part of the plan."

"It worked really well, though. You know. I run 'em out, you pummel them."

"Problem is, I never got to do any pummeling," he said, his voice rising a bit.

"Aww, baby. Do I sense a little jealousy?" Karla teased.

"Eww, I think I do," Lydia chimed.

Sebastian barked into his helmet. "Can it, Lydia. It's not jealousy."

"Oh, boy. I guess we'll be next. First, it was Brad and Angie, then Pratt and Faris," Karla said. "Neither could handle the rising stardom of their counterpart."

"No, no, no," Sebastian said, cutting her off. "First of all, Chris and Anna got back together. Second, Brad and Angelina never really got divorced."

Karla folded her arms across her chest. "Well, it sure as hell felt like it. I never got a sequel to *Mr. and Mrs. Smith.*"

"Whatever," Sebastian said. "And we didn't need a sequel to *Mr. and Mrs. Smith.* Thirdly, you're trying to make this out to be something it's not. We have to keep the team mentality if we are going to survive. Capes have all but disappeared. Thief is gone, and the few hero wannabes that did emerge quickly got wiped out by Mystikal and Mirage. Then they vanished. We have to move as a unit until others come. I let you run off and play rogue with the Majesties for a bit, but it's all about the two of us for now."

Karla nodded. "You're right. And I'll do better, baby."

"The mythos behind being a hero has changed quite a bit. Regular folks can do that. We have to be Super-Normals and that comes at a price. Whether we like it or not, our future depends on what we do every second we don these suits," Sebastian said.

"You've been reading Stelton's garbage again, huh?" Karla asked. "That man was an idiot."

"True, but *Curse the Capes* wasn't all bad. And it does put the way the others view us into perspective. We can all learn a little something from it," Sebastian said.

"I agree," Lydia said in a somewhat somber tone. "Things changed the moment people found out that Mr. Magnificent and Caine were the same person. The trust of the people has been dropped on its ear, and it's difficult to believe they'll sit upright again."

Sebastian sighed before putting his helmet back on. He took Blurr by the hands and gave a light squeeze. "Come on, baby. It's time we retire for the night."

Chapter 2
SPEED

The next day, Sebastian woke to an empty bed. He rolled to his side and found his slippers before grabbing his robe and bouncing downstairs. He was met by Karla, who was plopped on the couch in front of the television. Her body language—arms folded and legs scissored across the coffee table—screamed "Don't come near me," but he knew how to handle that just fine. He slid in next to her, tossed his arm around her neck, and planted a gentle kiss along her cheek. A reflexive smile burst across her face. "Hey, doll-baby. Did you sleep well?" he whispered, slowly moving his kisses down her neck.

Karla seemed preoccupied with something else, only answering him with a grunt. He turned to see what she was looking at. On the screen was a recap of their mob goon battle at the shipyard, courtesy of Daywatch. "Ugh, this high resolution shows all my pores," Karla said.

"Your pores? You can barely see anything on you as fast as you were moving last night, love."

"Yeah, maybe you can't see it, but my eyes track at—"

Sebastian rolled to his side and watched the ceiling. "About a thousand times the speed of a normal saccade. I know, Karla, you've only told me that a thousand times before."

"And what now? You're so used to me saying it that you're no longer amused? Impressed?"

His jaw dropped. "Are you really asking me that right now?"

Karla stood, arms folded. "Yes, I am, as a matter of fact," she nodded as if waiting for a response.

"I'm sorry, what were you asking me?"

"You heard me. Are you getting tired of me?" she asked.

There was an unfamiliar crack in her tone that cued him to the urgency of her words. She was fading fast. But why? "How could you ask me something like that, Karla?" Sebastian stood and held her by the waist. "I love you, you know that. That does not fade in time. Not when it's real."

"I know." Her eyes were glossy.

Sebastian softly rubbed the side of her cheek with the back of his hand. "What's really going on? You've been a bit on edge the last couple of days. Tell me what's on your mind."

When he finished speaking, he cupped her chin and lifted it with his fingers. Her eyes locked his. "It's not you, it's me."

"Oh, crap," he murmured. "Here it comes."

"No, I'm not breaking up with you, Sebas. It's not anything like that. I just... this is all so perfect. I know I don't deserve a guy like you." She looked around the room. "Or a place like this and a life of being a Hero. I'm a call-girl from the—"

Sebastian placed a finger over her lips. "Shhh, don't say another word. You are more than what you think of yourself, Karla. And certainly more than your past. We all have issues and skeletons."

"What skeletons do you have, Sebastian? You're practically a saint."

He smirked. She must've picked up on the insulted look on his face. "And I *dig* that about you, like *really* dig it. I needed someone like you in my life. But… it's hard to believe that it will all last. I feel so unworthy somehow. It's all…well…too perfect. I know it can't last forever. That's all. I anticipate the day that it will all go away."

"Hey," Sebastian said with his hands held chest high and his fingers splayed. "I'm no saint, and this is not heaven, nor is B.R.A.I.N. some sort of god."

"You called, Sebastian?" B.R.A.I.N. asked.

"No, I was just talking to Karla," Sebastian answered, looking at the ceiling as if the artificial intelligence would hear him any better by his doing so.

"Roger that," B.R.A.I.N. replied.

Sebastian turned his attention back to Karla. "I told you a while ago, no judgment here. I appreciate *everything* about you. The good, the bad, and the ugly. Your past is in the past. I knew the girl I fell in love with back in school was still out there waiting for me. She was trapped inside that lost woman who was running around with Dark Phase. Even then, when I found out what you were doing, there was nothing that could stop me from finding my way into your heart because you had already placed me in yours. I just needed time to get to you. My woman."

She blushed. "And that you did."

"That's right, I did. And I'm not letting go."

Karla slid into closer to him, resting her waist against him and hooking her leg around his. "You better not. Hear me?" Her voice was low and sultry.

"Not a chance, lady," Sebastian said in a whisper.

A whirlwind of kissing ensued, which led back to the bedroom and ended in an intimate moment that neither one of them would soon forget.

***

Later that day, Karla made a run to the grocery store to get something to cook for the night. She was somewhat of a phenom in the kitchen, darting back and forth between the stove, oven, refrigerator, and sink at lightning speed. Sebastian was always careful to steer clear as not to get run over. The idea of sneaker tread marks stamped across his forehead did little to encourage him to lend a hand.

Sebastian took the opportunity to lose himself in the upstairs laboratory while she was away. Plastered to his workstation, his mind was occupied with his latest experiment: the task of giving the S3 System a much-needed upgrade. "B.R.A.I.N., make preparations to run diagnostic test thirty-seven."

"You always say, 'Make preparations' as if I didn't know what you were doing in the first place and hadn't already done so."

"Right. It's a matter of semantics, B.R.A.I.N. I'm just doing the theatricality stuff. You know?"

"Not really."

"Just forget about it." Sebastian waved his hands. "Bring up the—"

Before he could finish, the room grew dark and a green wire-framed image of Sebastian's alter ego—Paladin—appeared, spinning slowly overhead in a newly-designed version of the S3. "Diagnostic test thirty-seven initiated," B.R.A.I.N. said.

Sebastian paced around the image, staring at it intently as if looking for some small detail that couldn't be seen with the naked eye. He stroked his chin before sliding on a pair of black gloves, trimmed in red along each digit, and with white circular padding in the palms. He then donned a pair of dark shades and raised his right hand in the direction of the suit.

His gloves pulsed in a bluish haze as he made contact with the image's foot, and he began to spin it clockwise. "S3.1 to your liking?" B.R.A.I.N. asked.

Sebastian answered with a nod. The new version of the S3 was almost identical to its predecessor with just a few minor enhancements that Sebastian was sure that only he and B.R.A.I.N. would notice. Rounded corners along the armor plating and the tighter bi-weave matrix that locked them in place made for a more streamlined design that would add more fluidity to Sebastian's movements—especially during brawls. Although that was all well and good, he had a deep-rooted wish to gain an aerodynamic edge over Blurr's acceleration capabilities. She'd shown him up one too many times over the past weeks during their chase-capades of running down criminals.

He pulled the image down and stared into the hollow eye sockets of the mask, face to face. "B.R.A.I.N.," he said over his shoulder. "It's to my liking, indeed."

"I thought you would approve."

Sebastian's eyes fell to the hollowed socket on Paladin's chest where one of the three breastplate attachments usually go, and his hands reflexively moved to his pocket. He pulled out a small disc no larger than the size of a quarter and pointed it at the breastplate. A red laser pierced the center and began to construct a new breastplate, quickly filling the space. Moments later, it was done and Sebastian took a few steps back to admire his creation with folded arms. "I like it a lot, as a matter of fact."

The breastplate was a mash-up of sorts, doing away with all of the previous separate attachments and replacing them with one solitary image: an S intertwined with the number three.

"Diagnostics report, B.R.A.I.N.," Sebastian said.

"It's early, but everything seems to be functioning nominally. The new attachment seems to be holding up just fine. The weight is perfect and the internal CPU is running along without a hitch. It's virtually purring," B.R.A.I.N. said, drawing an obvious reference to Blurr's former Cheetah persona.

Sebastian slammed his fist into his palm. "I knew it! It was only a matter of time until I figured it out."

"*You* figured it out?"

"Well, *we* figured it out, of course."

"*We?*" B.R.A.I.N. replied.

"I mean, you did, but I helped. It was more like a fifty/fifty split."

"Try eighty/twenty."

"Sixty/forty."

"Seventy/thirty."

"Okay, sixty-five/thirty-five!" Sebastian said, his voice rising.

"No, ninety/ten," B.R.A.I.N. said.

"Hey, how did the numbers go back up? I was successfully talking you down. You know, negotiating."

"I'm an artificial intelligence, Sebastian. I don't need to negotiate."

Sebastian shook his head and stepped in closer to the image of the S3.1 once more. "It doesn't matter. All that matters is that we're ready... again."

"The single breastplate design will prevent you from having to limit your powers to a mission-by-mission basis from now on—or rely on Lydia to send you a new variant in the heat of battle. You should be able to switch modes on the fly now. There is a slight delay, though. Limited only by your human thought processing speed."

"Excellent, that's what I was hoping for. Hey, wait a minute. There's nothing slow about my processing speed."

"Stymie your pride, Sebastian. You're about one-eighth the capacity of maximal processes that I can assimilate at just fifty percent."

"Okay. Point taken. What are the chances of the suit holding up this time?"

"Promising."

"Promising? I need a little more than that, B.R.A.I.N."

"Getting *cold* feet? Where's your faith, Sebas?"

"Very funny," Sebastian said, pointing to an overhead monitor. "That malfunction over Lake Michigan was not my fault. I had the flu for a week thanks to you. Bad play on words, by the way."

"Ahh, you know you loved it," B.R.A.I.N. said.

The lights turned back on and the wire-framed image disappeared. Sebastian removed his shades and began to do the same to his gloves. "Get Lydia on the comms."

"Sure thing. And I'll start production on the Prototype and upload the new enhancements as soon as possible."

"New enhancements?" Sebastian asked.

"I took the liberty of making a few tweaks myself. Upon further analysis of your performances over the last few months, I compared desired versus actual outcomes and, by and large, you left a lot on the field of play."

"Hey!" Sebastian yelled.

"But don't you worry; they're minor modifications that should offer you a distinct tactical advantage. You'll thank me. Trust me."

"And what data did you have to go on? Need I remind you who saved this city?"

A female voice piped in, saying, "Need I remind *you*?"

"Ms. Lydia is on the comms," B.R.A.I.N. said, an air of sarcasm in its voice.

"This isn't over, B.R.A.I.N.," Sebastian said, looking at the ceiling. "Shut it down for a while, will you? Save some energy." He turned his

19

attention back to his cousin. "Hey, Lydia," he said finally, fully removing his gloves and walking them back over to his workstation.

"Hey, cousin," Lydia replied. "So, whatcha doing?"

"Just running some tests and tinkering."

"The mouse will play while the cat's away, huh," Lydia teased.

"She's not Cheetah-Girl anymore," Sebastian barked.

"Come on, Sebas, I was just playing. What's up your butt?"

Sebastian sighed. "Sorry, Lydia. I'm just a little perturbed, that's all."

"From what? Isn't life with my favorite Super-heroine lovely as always? When are you going to make an honest woman out of her?"

"I'd like to. Trust me. But—"

"But what?" Lydia interrupted. "You shouldn't waste time, Sebas. We're not promised tomorrow, you know."

"I know. It's just… I'm not sure if she's fully onboard yet, you know? I don't want her to just be here because it's convenient. I want her to really *want* to be here."

"Well, you can't blame the girl for thinking of herself first. She's had a pretty crummy life thus far, and her choices of men have been lousy at best. Taking up a relationship with a low key millionaire genius isn't a bad gig."

Sebastian's face lit up. "Did you say genius?"

"No."

"No, I distinctly heard you call me a billionaire genius, didn't you, B.R.A.I.N.?" Sebastian asked.

"I don't know. I was too busy shutting down and saving energy for a while. Need I remind *you*," B.R.A.I.N. answered.

Sebastian boiled. "Err," he grunted.

"Like I was saying," Lydia interjected, "women love security. And you're in a pretty secure situation. I'm sure that attracted her at first and, now that she's had a moment to settle in, she's probably evaluating you to see if this is the real deal and if you're really what she needs and wants."

"Did you talk to her or something?" Sebastian asked.

"No."

"Then how do you know so much?"

"Because, silly, all women think like this. It's instinct. Men need sex, toys, and admiration out of a relationship, and women really just need one thing: security. The toys and sex kinda go together so we can eliminate the middle man."

"Ha, ha. Very funny. But seriously. I'm worried about her. She still feels very... how do I say it?"

"Insecure," B.R.A.I.N. added.

"Oh, Mr. Shutdown is back, huh," Sebastian teased.

"Hard to fully shut down when the both of you are in my space," B.R.A.I.N. said. "And talking about my favorite Super-Normal at that."

"Since when was she your favorite?" Sebastian asked.

"She's everybody's favorite, Sebas. Duh," Lydia said. "Anyway, I was thinking. I haven't seen you since like, what, yesterday? I wanted to swing by."

Sebastian folded his arms. "Well, everybody's *favorite* Super-Normal isn't here. You'd be wasting time if you came by now."

"Sen... si... tive, are we?" Lydia teased. "My god. We all know you're my *favorite*... cousin."

"Last I checked, wasn't I the only cousin?"

"No, we have some more family on the west coast. We just never see them, that's all."

"Hey Lydia, what's the chances they're Super-Normals? Wouldn't that be cool?"

"Funny you should say that. I grabbed a few articles off the Super Hero fan sites about that new Super-Normal named Menzuo. He's young, but he's kinda cute. I'd like to see him up close, you know? Maybe he's family. He reminds me of you a little."

"That guy's a real fireball from what I've heard. Not tamable at all and probably not a good fit for what we're doing. Just how does he remind you of me?" Sebastian asked.

"Nothing in particular, but I see a slight resemblance in the eyes."

"His eyes are stark white. What are you talking about? Besides, I'm not all that sure he's on our side. Rumor has it he's a real alien. Who knows why he's here in the first place."

"Sebastian has a point," B.R.A.I.N. interjected. "All the references I've found on Menzuo trace his heritage to deep space. It's mostly conjecture, but he's definitely not from our solar system—possibly not even our galaxy."

"Well, either way, he's a cutie," Lydia said.

22

"And he's a child. We need men and women to fight, not kids. Speaking of which, Blurr said that the Majesties of Canaan were pretty cool. And some of the men are closer to your age bracket, Lydia. I might know a guy…or two, or three."

"Ha, ha. I'll pass. Military types bore me. Anyhow, I'll be en route soon. Finishing up a few work items," Lydia said.

Sebastian's eyebrows bunched. "A few work items. What are you talking about? You work for me?"

"Yeah, that's right. And I'm working on a few things *for* you."

"Things of interest, I'm sure, right?"

"Of course. Need I remind you *who* saved this city," Lydia said sarcastically.

"Touché," Sebastian said. "See you soon, cousin."

B.R.A.I.N. cut the comms and Sebastian walked back over to the workstation. He waved his hand over the front screen and an image of the new S3.1 materialized, along with a bar graph next to it, approximately one-third of the way full. The number next to it was thirty. "Coming along nicely, huh, B.R.A.I.N.?"

"I should have a prototype ready for testing soon. Give it a few days."

"Great. I'm gonna take a quick nap before Lydia gets here. Wake me up if she or Karla arrives."

"Will do."

***

Hours later, Sebastian found himself in a crazy dream. He stood overlooking a vast field of black glass and the sky was filled with nothing but red clouds and white stars. Lightning cracked overhead, but no sounds of thunder interrupted the silence.

Sebastian watched as an object approached in the distance, moving at an amazing speed. A cloud of broken glass swirled in its wake as it zipped along the ground. As it got closer, the object became more distinguishable. It was Karla, but she wasn't adorned in any Super-Normal costume, just a pair of spandex shorts and a sports bra.

"Karla," he muttered as she slowed and came to a complete stop before him. Her eyes sparkled like diamonds and her body cast a faint, ghostly image around her that seemed to vibrate in rhythm with her breathing.

"Yes, my love. I am your queen," she said as she held out her hand to him. "Come with me, my king. We have much work to do."

"Karla, what is this place?"

She flashed a mischievous grin. "I can't tell you just yet. But you need to come with me."

Sebastian took Karla's hand. "I can't just follow you without an explanation. This place," Sebastian said, amazedly looking around, "it isn't home."

"No, it's not. But you have to come with me quickly before they come. If we wait, it may be too late. I only have a small window." Karla tugged harder on Sebastian's hand to coerce him to leave, but

24

Sebastian stood his ground.

"No, Karla. And who is coming?"

Just then, the sky opened, the red canvas parted like a zipper. "It's too late," she said.

Dozens of gigantic ships entered the atmosphere and descended upon them. As one solo ship broke from the others and closed in, Sebastian started doing the pulling, attempting to run and drag Karla in the opposite direction. But Karla snatched away and stood in anticipation of whatever was about to happen as if she was expecting something.

"Karla," Sebastian screamed.

A light pierced the sky, emanating from the nosecone of the ship and bathing Karla in a shower of dazzling lights. Karla closed her eyes and held her arms at her side. Sebastian crashed in and tore her from the light just before a red laser beam scorched the ground before them. Sebastian stood, this time donning the S3.1 suit.

The ship fired the red laser again, but this time, instead of retreating, Paladin initiated the strength mode of the suit, deflected the beam with his forearm shield, and aimed it back in the direction of the ship. The beam split the ship into pieces, and it erupted into a dazzling explosion as smoke filled the sky. Paladin turned to check on Karla but she was gone, lifted away by a scout ship that had slipped in behind him.

Paladin switched to speed mode and raced into the sky after the ship, closing the distance between them. He let out a scream as he pumped his arms harder, willing his legs to follow. He grabbed ahold of the hull door and ripped it free, revealing an unconscious Karla inside. Just as he stretched his arm to grab her, a sensation of heat spread throughout his back and he paused in a panic, realizing that a second ship had caught up with him and penetrated the weakest part of his suit with another blast.

The pain was excruciating and exacting. Paladin could feel his skin cooking, surely having lost anything resembling flesh and muscle at this point. He turned and shielded himself from the blast and gunned toward the ship, making quick work of it with a few well-timed super-speed punches and kicks. The ship crumbled under his barrage and Paladin made haste to catch back up with Karla.

But it was too late.

Karla was gone, along with any remnants of the fleet. Paladin lost all feeling in his body as he drifted back toward the earth below. After falling for what seemed like an eternity, he finally splashed down to the ground with a thud.

Sebastian awakened from his dream, dripping in sweat. He searched the bed for Karla, but no one was there. He jumped from his bed and ran down the stairs, stopping quickly as he was alerted to the sound of chatter coming from the kitchen. It was Karla and Lydia, carrying on a conversation about who knows what. All that mattered was that Karla was wearing a smile—a far stretch from what he saw in his tortuous dream.

"Made it back, love?" Sebastian asked.

Karla turned to find him. "Yeah, I hope we didn't wake you."

"I know you wanted me to call you when Karla got back, but she made me promise to leave you to napping instead." Lydia held up a glass of wine. "Well, that was after she offered me a glass of Merlot as a bribe. Couldn't resist," Lydia said with a smile.

Sebastian approached Karla and planted a soft kiss on her cheek. Karla must've felt the passion in his touch. "What was that for, baby?"

"Nothing. I just missed you, that's all," he replied.

"Aww, you guys are so sweet," Lydia said.

Karla touched his cheek and returned the gesture.

"Should I be leaving now?" Lydia asked before scarfing down another long sip of her wine.

"No, of course not," Karla said. "Lydia was just telling me about some new fluctuations in seismic activity. Similar to those recorded around the time of the Storm. Could possibly be new Super-Normals."

"Are you sure, Lydia?" Sebastian asked.

"Maybe. But B.R.A.I.N. is usually never wrong," Lydia replied.

"I'm never wrong," B.R.A.I.N. retorted.

"God, I wish we could mute him sometimes," Sebastian said.

"Shh, Sebas," Lydia said. "He's sensitive. I've been working on his emotional algorithms."

"Mind if I ask why?" Sebastian asked.

"Well, I theorize that the more humanistic B.R.A.I.N. gets, the more intuitive he'll become with predicting Super-Normal—specifically villainous—activity," Lydia said in a whisper.

Sebastian shook his head. "Suit yourself. But we'll never have a private conversation again."

"At least he does give us a little privacy during our *alone* time," Karla said.

Sebastian nodded. "That's because I damped his scanning range in our bedroom once you moved in, remember? Lined the room with lead plating."

"He's not interested in your shenanigans, guys," Lydia said.

"Anyway," Sebastian said, raising his voice to a more normal level. "What about these possible Super-Normals? We haven't had much activity lately. Just regular mobsters and robbers."

"I'm not quite sure, but the energy surges are off the charts. The fluctuations are not localized either. Skips around the city. Very hard to trace it. It's like it's teleporting from location to location, but not in a predictable pattern. If it is a Super-Normal, it's one bad dude," Lydia cautioned.

"That reminds me, I've made some modifications to the S3. Upgraded it to S3.1 status earlier today. B.R.A.I.N. said it should be ready in a few days. I'd like to take it for a spin." He looked over to Karla. "You up for a little morning run, baby?"

"A few days, not hours," B.R.A.I.N. barked over the speakers.

"Nothing's stopping us from a beta test here and there. It will help you further work out the bugs, B.R.A.I.N.," Sebastian replied.

"Only the speed modification is available now, anyway. So it couldn't hurt. But bring it back in one piece," B.R.A.I.N. said.

Sebastian smiled. "Of course." He looked over to Karla. "So?"

Karla winked at him. "Always. What'd you have in mind?"

"Lydia, do your best to pinpoint a signal trace of the possible Super-Normal," Sebastian said, flashing a hit of bravado that excited Karla, evident by the blush saturating her cheeks. " Make your best guestimate, triangulate a radius of about two or three miles out from that, and give me the coordinates in the morning. Karla and I will play around in the vicinity for a bit, speeding through the city, putting the S3.1 through its paces. My hunch is that our new friend will show themselves when we do."

"Will do," Lydia said.

"What makes you so sure they'll show?" asked Karla.

"Easy. Everybody loves a game of hide and seek," Sebastian said.

Chapter 3
lightning

Daylight slashed between the tall, arching skyscrapers of the Chicago skyline, almost blinding to the naked eye. But it had no effect on Paladin, whose newly-designed headgear now sported a set of internal ultraviolet ray-shading goggles that automatically activated when exposed to sudden fluctuations in temperature and color hues of the visual spectrum. Admittedly, he'd swiped the idea from the technology interlaced in Blurr's spectacles.

She was now some ten paces in front of him and opening the distance with each footfall. It was less about his lack of speed that kept him in second place but more about his insatiable desire to fiddle with the various newly designed, heads-up displays before him.

"B.R.A.I.N. and Lydia weren't lying when they said they had a few upgrades," Paladin said as he rounded the corner of Lewis and Faircloth.

"Oh, yeah. You enjoying the view from back there, lover boy?" Blurr teased.

"Being behind you never gets old, baby. You know that."

Blurr hesitantly looked back at him with a blush as his facial scanning tech quickly locked in on her and identified her, placing an older headshot of Karla in the upper right-hand corner of his display. "I see that smile, girl."

"Well, indulge while you can. I'm about to burn," Blurr said, and she skipped across three buildings so fast that Paladin swore her feet never landed.

As she cleared the three structures, a targeting reticle darted along each building in a similar path, just offset the same route that Blurr took. The words OPTIMAL ROUTE highlighted the center. Paladin followed the trail perfectly, shaving off approximately two seconds in the process. Before he knew it, he'd closed within three steps of Blurr by the time they'd hit the next building.

He pulled alongside her and gave a salute. "What," Blurr said.

"Yeah, I know. I can't resist the burn."

A pair of E.I.Es joined them, hovering about fifty feet above them. The S3 wasn't the only thing Sebastian had upgraded. With the increased Super-Normal activity worldwide and the murmurs of unseen visitors from other galaxies looming ahead, Chicago had recently benefited from a bump in its homeland security budget, allowing more R&D to be thrown at the usage of drones for surveillance. And, quite naturally, Sabastian had put in for a grant or two of his own to increase the zoomed fidelity of the cameras and the engine speed of his artificial private eyes.

"Looking good, guys," Paladin said, noticing their presence.

"Please don't talk to them," Blurr said.

"Why not?"

"Because."

"Because what? Because it's cool?"

31

"No, because it's weird. A grown man shouldn't be talking to toys."

"Well, I tend to not think of them as toys. They are more like friends."

Blurr shook her head. "Like imaginary ones."

"No, like real ones. They have feelings, you know. I programmed them that way."

Blurr raced along the side of Willis Tower—the tallest building in Chicago—until hitting the rooftop. She grabbed the side of the rooftop with both hands and somersaulted her way to the top, landing feet first in a half-knee position. "Now you're scaring me."

Paladin mimicked her maneuver and landed about three feet ahead of her, standing. He offered her a hand. "You should really try to get to know them."

Blurr swatted his hand away. "I'll pass."

"You're not jealous, are you?"

"I'm annoyed. You just passed me," she said.

Paladin pointed at the right temple. "Sorry, upgraded NAV Projection System."

"The N.P.S.," Lydia said over the comms. "Performing well."

"I see," Blurr said.

Paladin and Blurr walked to the edge of Willis Tower and looked over. The city never looked so brilliant. The glimmer of the sun refracted from each building below caught every spectral color the human eye could recognize, from light reds to navy blues and burnt oranges to dazzling yellows. The cars below skated by in perfect precision, like the second hand on a clock.

"Crazy, isn't it?" Paladin murmured. "How life just seems to make sense from up here. As if it's all working along some path of predestination."

"It is," Blurr added.

"How are you feeling, Sebastian?" B.R.A.I.N. asked.

"Fine. I feel more than fine. The S3.1 is holding up well under the speed stresses," Paladin said.

"And the temperature?" B.R.A.I.N. asked.

'What about it?" Paladin replied.

"I picked up slight increases in your thermal temperature throughout your route. I don't want the suit to overheat," B.R.A.I.N. said.

"I hadn't noticed," Paladin said.

Blurr turned to face him, slid her hands around his waist, and pressed her body against his. "How's he doing now, B.R.A.I.N.? Is he getting hot?"

The E.I.Es swooped in closer.

"Still performing for the camera, honey?" Paladin asked.

"No. Only for my man," she whispered. Blurr looked up and smiled at the closest drone. "But I am looking for a new lipstick sponsor if anyone's offering."

"His temperature is—"

B.R.A.I.N. was suddenly cut off by the sound of an explosion in the distance. Blurr's and Paladin's heads whipped to the direction of the noise as a building came crashing down on itself. What appeared to be a bolt of lightning burst upward from beneath the rubble and began to hover hundreds of feet above the ground.

As if upon command, the E.I.Es immediately raced toward the flashing object as a giant blimp, affixed with a Jumbotron screen along the side of it lit up. As the cameras zoomed in on the lighting image, a woman surrounded in a glimmering ball of electricity materialized.

"Citizens of Chicago, the death bell has been runggggg," she said in a theatrical tone as if she was singing. "Once I've killed everyone here, I will make my way to the stratosphereeeeeeeeee!"

"What the hell?" Paladin asked as he sped into action, trailing Blurr on a collision course with the strange woman. They pulled up short, coming to a halt on an adjacent rooftop building. Paladin pointed at her and cried out for her attention. "This madness stops here. Surrender now and... and..." He paused and looked over at Blurr, searching for the right words to say. The woman turned her toward them and flashed a cold smile.

"Someone you know?" Blurr asked.

"No," Paladin replied.

"Spit it out then," Blurr whispered.

"I'm not sure what to say. I've never encountered a mad... *woman* before."

Blurr shook her head and stepped forward. "Hey, chica, drop down or get hurt. This madness has to stop."

"Well, well, well. If it isn't Traitor Nation," she said calmly.

"Traitor Nation?" Paladin asked.

"Yes, you two have left your destiny and sided with a dying breed. These Normals need to die so that we can live!" Her voice boomed.

Blurr covered her ears and writhed to a knee. Paladin held his ground, safely shielded by his helmet and unaffected by the noise.

The woman gawked at him, appearing somewhat surprised he was still standing. "Why don't you kneel too?" she sang again, raising her voice once again.

This sent Blurr completely prostrate. Paladin fumed, quickly grabbed a loose brick from the ground, and tossed it at the hovering woman at full speed. Although there was no way she could've been quick enough to avoid the assault, she didn't have to as she instantly incinerated the brink by surrounding herself with an electric bubble.

The woman laughed. "Foolish Super-Normal. Your fate is sealed tooooooooooooo!"

The time she took to speak was just enough to allow Blurr to regain her footing and launch at the woman. But instead of punching through the protective electric shield, she bounced off like a ping pong ball, hurling into a nearby building.

"I hate opera," Paladin yelled just as he made his approach. Skating across the sky, he closed the distance between himself and the woman in nanoseconds and slammed into the electric bubble with similar results; Paladin was repelled into the rubble of the building beneath them.

The woman laughed aloud. "No one, Normal or Super-Normal, is a match for Dame Lightninggggg!"

Paladin peeled himself from the debris below and stood, watching as Dame Lightning flung multiple volleys of lightning bolts at normal spectators. Eight to ten innocent bystanders burst into flames at Lightning's hands.

"Stop," Paladin yelled.

Dame Lightning gazed down on Paladin, her eyes gleaming wildly in a red haze, reflecting on her baby blue unitard. Her all-white head of long hair stood straight up as though it were consumed by static electricity. "I'm only helping them in their evolution. We've excelled, and they are decaying. It was only a matter of time. Every organism must make the leap to survive. The Normals have remained stagnant for much too long. Now, it is our—I mean, *my* timeeeeeee!" She raised her right hand and aimed at another civilian hiding behind a tree. Paladin bolted in front of the Normal, absorbed the full brunt of the lightning, and launched forward, plowing through the tree and into an adjacent wall. Fortunately, the person was unharmed and quickly escaped down an alleyway.

Before Paladin could stand, Dame Lightning was upon him, tossing more electric volleys his way. But this time, he was ready, quickly evading her attacks and parrying a few body shots in the process; he had realized that she could not both maintain the electric barrier and throw lightning at the same time. He had his newly upgraded N.P.S. to thank for that.

Blurr picked up on it too, zooming in and raining down multiple roundhouse kicks that connected with Dame Lightning's head, shoulder, and trunk—the last one bouncing Dame Lightning to the street below. The electric shield dissipated. Paladin and Blurr circled the woman, cautious not to approach too quickly.

"See, she's not that impressive," Paladin said sarcastically.

"I know you think you're doing the right thing, but you're not. Evolution is a natural thing and we must help the Normals into the next phase," Dame Lightning pleaded.

"By killing us? I'm afraid not," Paladin replied.

Dame Lightning smirked. "I knew you were not one of us," she said as she rose to her feet. "Under that super suit you're just some simple Normal, aren't you? Probably some rich playboy with a dozen fast cars, fancy toys, and no place to go," Dame Lightning teased.

"You sure you don't know her? I hate crazy exes, you know. Nothing more irritating," Blurr said.

"Do I look like I date crazy women with checkered pasts?" Paladin asked. Blurr cut her eyes at him. Paladin raised a finger at her. "Don't answer that!"

Dame Lightning clasped her hands together and the sky turned dark. A small funnel began to lower from the clouds above, lifting cars and loose trash toward the sky. "Now I will destroy this city, my oh my oh my, what a pityyyyyyy!"

"Crap, shield is back up," Blurr said.

"Okay. So she can make tornados and maintain shields. I'm a little impressed now," Paladin admitted.

"Now," Blurr said, eyebrows raised.

Dame Lighting released her grip and fanned her hands in a circle before extending her arms out front. The funnel shot forth, tearing through the street and leaving a fissure along the ground in its wake. Pedestrians fled as the funnel lifted vehicles, trash cans, and just about anything in its path.

"Why do they always stay around longer than they should?" Blurr asked as she sprinted ahead of the funnel and zigzagged from sidewalk to sidewalk, scooping up lagging onlookers and safely placing them out of harm's way on opened buildings one to two blocks away.

"Good job, Blurr. I'll take Dame," Paladin shouted over the comms. As he turned to find Dame Lightning, he was pummeled by a large object that flung him into the side of a glass bus stop post. He landed on his back and slowly began to peel himself from the pavement.

"Sebas," Lydia screamed over the comms.

"I'm fine." He winced as he stood, making his best effort to locate Dame Lightning.

"You're not in the strength suit," Lydia said. "You're vulnerable."

Paladin's N.P.S. replicated a NAV trajectory of the best-anticipated route to find and flank Dame Lightning. Without a moment's hesitation, he followed the path to perfection and, seconds later, found himself standing behind a large water feature shadowing Dame Lightning. Unaware of his presence, Dame Lightning had lowered her shield momentarily and was talking with someone over a small inner earpiece. "I've got them. Yes… they are easier targets than you assumed. The hooker will die tonight. I promise."

Paladin watched as Dame Lightning set her sights on Blurr, who had just returned to rescue one last Normal—an old lady prostrate along the ground. As she knelt over the woman to gently help her up, Dame Lightning took aim.

Rage flooded Paladin's body, and before he knew it, as if being pulled along by a string, his body simultaneously trailed a new path generated by the N.P.S. straight for Dame Lightning. In seconds, he slammed his fist through her back at full speed. In an instant, he withdrew his hand and, as it slowed just enough to visualize, a bleeding heart pulsated beneath his fingertips.

Dame Lightning dropped to the floor like a ragdoll and the storm immediately dissipated, the dark clouds rolled back, and the sun returned. Blurr cleared the old lady from the area and found her way to Paladin, who knelt beside Dame Lightning's body.

Blurr cupped his shoulders. "You did it," she whispered.

"Yeah, I did."

The crowd of Normals began to swell as they surrounded the two heroes, pelting them with cheers.

"Time for you guys to book it," Lydia said over the comms. "B.R.A.I.N. says the S3.1 needs to recharge."

Blurr roused Paladin to stand. "Come on, baby, we got to go."

Paladin nodded and dropped Dame Lightning's heart to the floor. Blurr joined hands with him, raised their fists to the sky, and momentarily reveled in the crowd's appreciation.

Then, just as soon as they appeared, they sped away.

Chapter 4
thoughts

Paladin chewed aimlessly on his bottom lip as the warm water droplets of the shower pummeled his sore frame. The last fall he suffered from Dame Lightning's wind blast had taken more of a toll on him than he initially realized. A large bruise along half of his back painted a purple and red explosion similar to a butterfly's wings—or more akin to the wings of an angel, per Lydia's description.

The S3.1 had performed rather admirably. Utilizing the speed variant and once again, Paladin had successfully repelled another evil Super-Normal attack on New Chicago. But he couldn't summon the strength to partake in the celebration that was waiting for him when he arrived back at his penthouse suite between Lydia and Karla.

How could he? He had killed another person. Again.

The body counts were slowly rising over the last few months as his heroic effort to protect the city came at the expense of wiping out resistant superhumans. The image of Dame Lightning's limp body crumbling to the floor was a stain that would not soon be scrubbed clean from his mind. The visual of her still-ticking heart pulsating in his hand was most likely engraved in his memories forever. In some twisted feat to repent for his sins, he absorbed the hot water of his shower—which was also infused with antiseptic meds—in the small lacerations along his body, a failed attempt to purge the memory of her last moments.

Lydia had taken the S3.1 from and safely tucked it away in the storage capsule for final modifications and repairs as he separated himself from the alter ego of Paladin upon entering his abode. Karla and Lydia had respectfully given him his space and remained downstairs as he sulked alone.

After washing away what was left of his guilt, he slipped out of the shower and donned a robe before joining the ladies back downstairs.

Lydia approached him and gave her cousin a firm hug. A handful of narcotic drugs had done a sufficient job of numbing his body so her outpouring of love didn't hurt as much.

"You okay?" Lydia asked, meeting his eyes.

"Yeah, I'm fine," he replied.

Karla was next, planting a kiss on his forehead and handing him a steaming cup of Chai tea. She walked him over to the couch and sat down next to him, resting her head on his shoulder. Lydia squatted down on a loveseat across from them, sitting Indian style. "So, that was pretty strange, huh?"

"What was strange?" Sebastian asked.

"That opera singing Super-Normal," Lydia pressed. "I ran a diagnostic search on some of the DNA from the blood on the S3.1 —"

"Maybe not now," Karla said.

"I'm fine, Karla. I've made peace with it. What'd you find, Lydia?" Sebastian asked.

"Silly me. It can wait until tomorrow," Lydia said.

"No," Sebastian snapped. "If it's important, it's better I know now rather than later."

"Okay," Lydia said, hesitantly staring at Karla for approval.

"Go ahead," Karla said.

Lydia nodded. "Well, it appears that Dame Lightning's real name was Sarah Tolbert, a forty-two-year-old ex-migrant worker who quit her job three years ago and followed her passion as an opera singer. She struggled at first to find her path but eventually broke through and made a nice go of it, touring in various stage plays across the country. She even booked a few smaller roles on Broadway."

"Okay, I'm missing how this is so strange. Plenty of people hit a midlife crisis and follow their passions," Sebastian said.

"You didn't let me finish," Lydia said. "Want to know how a psychopath works, what do you look at first in her private records?"

"I don't know, dating history?" Karla asked.

"No, silly. You check their bank accounts," Lydia said.

"Lydia," Sebastian yelled.

"I didn't do it, B.R.A.I.N. did. Blame him," Lydia said.

"I hardly think that I should take the full brunt of the responsibility here as I was only following the direction of my end-user," B.R.A.I.N. said.

"Traitor," Lydia said. "Anyway, fine, I did ask B.R.A.I.N. to do it. But, it was for the protection of the city. The greater good. That's what we signed up for, right?"

"Go on," Sebastian said finally.

"Well, it appears that over the last six months, Sarah was receiving random deposits in her bank accounts from an untraceable source. Not chump change, mind you. Tens of thousands of dollars. B.R.A.I.N. tried to tack the routing numbers of the wired deposits, but they pinged through millions of gateways that eventually ended up...well...in space," Lydia said.

"In space?" Karla asked.

"Yes. I didn't believe it myself but, when B.R.A.I.N. pulled up the coordinates, all of the deposits landed on an asteroid just outside the rings of Saturn."

"That's insane," Sebastian said.

"No, it's strange," Lydia said.

"Right." Sebastian stopped to take a sip of his tea. "It's strange."

"Finally!" Lydia said.

"So, any ideas as to what that could mean?" Sebastian asked.

Lydia scratched her head. "Not sure. But I am nursing a theory or two. Mainly, she must have been a gun for hire, sent here to kill Normals—possibly to offset the current peaceful relationship between Normals and Super-Normals in New Chicago since the big fallout with Caine and Dark Phase."

"Or to just kill good Super-Normals. She wasn't discriminating out there tonight," Karla said.

Sebastian chimed in. "I think it may be deeper than that. When I snuck up behind her, she was communicating with someone over her inner earpiece device. She said, 'I've got them. Yes... they are easier targets than you assumed.' *You.* She was very specific. Only one other person of interest."

"See, it was a hit job," Lydia said, seemingly pleased with herself.

"No, there's more. She was chanting some mumbo jumbo about humans not evolving and it being the job of Super-Normals to help them along," Sebastian said.

"Well, that was nice of her," Lydia said.

"She meant evolution through death," Karla said.

"Oh…not good then," Lydia said. "Well, do you think aliens are planning some attack on planet Earth?"

"I doubt it. Probably just some tracking worm program meant to confuse anyone trying to get a fix on their signal. A ghosting software," Sebastian said.

"And I doubt aliens pay in U.S. dollars," Karla added.

"Well, we better figure out something soon. We certainly can't afford anymore hate-mongering on the planet. There isn't any room for it. Humans already do a sizeable job of hating one another for differences of color, ethnicity, sexuality, and gender. Can you imagine if we start separating ourselves based on special gifts?"

"Is she totally wrong in her thinking?" Karla asked.

"What? Of course, she is," Sebastian said.

"Don't be so defensive," Karla said. "Think about it. The human race is an immutable killer. We ravage animals and other species into virtual extinction time and time again. We don't learn. We just keep doing whatever the hell we want. Whatever we deem necessary. Maybe it's time someone else does the extinguishing for a change to make us wake up."

"So what, does that include us too?" Lydia asked.

Karla placed her hand on top of Lydia's. "Not entirely. I don't mean everyone should suffer, just those bigoted A-holes at the top of the food chain who don't give a damn about anyone else on the planet. They need to feel what it's like to be at the bottom of the totem pole for once."

"I feel the frustration too, Karla. But it wouldn't be right to go on some mercy killing-spree because we feel that it evens the playing field. We can't want change so badly that we now conform to extreme measures. It doesn't make us any better than they are," Sebastian said.

"Perhaps we need an off-world solution to our problems. I bet you Menzuo could help us," Lydia teased with a smile.

"Sorry, Lydia, I don't feel like entertaining children. I told you, we need men and women." Sebastian turned from Lydia and looked Karla's way. "Is it possible to connect back with the Majesties of Canaan?" he asked.

"I could reach out if they're not too busy. I know Slaycick told me they were exploring a new lead somewhere in the Middle East," Karla said.

Sebastian raised an eyebrow. "When did you speak to him?"

"He messaged me on social media," Karla said.

"What!" Sebastian said in a high-pitched tone.

"Call down, love-birds. We have bigger fish to fry," Lydia said.

"Focus. We need answers, not bickering."

Sebastian was fuming inside but didn't let his jealously get the best of him. "Fine. After Karla reaches out, we should be able to get a better handle on our current state."

"So what then? We just hold tight for now?" Karla asked.

"It's the best we can do," Lydia said. "It's not like we're in some state of emergency. We're crime fighters and protectors of New Chicago, not some world organization. Our directives haven't been altered."

Sebastian turned away. "Yeah, tell that to Sarah Tolbert's family."

Karla walked over and hugged Sebastian from behind. "You can't feel down about it, baby. She chose that path and was trying to harm a lot of people. You had no choice."

"I know," he whispered. "It just sucks that there wasn't another way."

As Karla was about to speak, there was a knock at the door.

"You guys expecting company?" Lydia asked.

"No," Sebastian said.

"More importantly, how'd they get by the bellhop, doorman, and the front desk without them alerting us?" Sebastian asked.

"I smell trouble," Karla said, moving into a defensive stance with her hands fisted at her sides.

Sebastian eyed the stairs to the laboratory. If he ran now in an attempt to get to the S3.1, he'd leave the girls defenseless. But if he stayed, he risked being absolutely worthless to defend them without the   suit.

"B.R.A.I.N.," he cried out.

"Already on it," B.R.A.I.N. answered as a boom erupted from upstairs. What followed was the S3.1 sailing over the stair railing and falling onto the couch across the room. Karla zipped into action and whisked both Sebastian and the S3.1 off into the bathroom behind the kitchen. Sebastian closed his eyes to avoid motion sickness. It was an entirely different experience to run fast on your own versus someone carrying you at the speed of light. When he opened them again, the S3.1 was in his hands and Karla had made the transition to her alter ego, Blurr.

"Suit up. I'll hold off whoever it is at the door. And don't worry, I ran Lydia's upstairs too," Blurr said.

Sebastian nodded and began swapping out his clothing for the S3.1. Just as he donned his pants, there was a subsequent knock at the door. "Karla," Sebastian cried inquisitively. When she failed to answer, he paused and ran around the corner as his heart raced in his chest. "Karla!"

When he rounded the corner, he was met by a handful of military soldiers in camo gear sporting handguns and rifles, along with a tall black man wearing a blue suit, holding his hat in his hands. The left side of his chest was adorned in about thirty medals. Sebastian covered half his face with his hands and scanned the room for Blurr.

"Take your hand down, son. We already know your identity," the man said. Sebastian lowered his hand and spotted Blurr standing off to the side with a curious grin on her face. "I'm Colonel Daren Matheson of the United States Army, and we have been sent by the president of our great country to have a word with you and your team."

Paladin removed the last of the S3.1 torso and arm gear and motioned Colonel Matheson over to the couch. "We're all ears."

Colonel Matheson, Blurr, Lydia, and Paladin settled in around the coffee table and took a seat, Paladin and Blurr on the couch next to the Colonel and Lydia on the loveseat.

"First of all, I want to thank you all for your efforts against Caine," Matheson began. "He was becoming a real threat to national security. We had been watching him for quite a while and, like you, Paladin, we couldn't figure out how he was so entrenched in the operations of both sides. He always seemed one step ahead of everyone else. There was definitely some collusion there as well, but it was obvious that we were missing another piece."

"The dual identity of Mr. Magnificent," Paladin said.

Matheson pointed at Paladin. "Right! You all took him out, and we are grateful. Even if we did figure it out, there was nothing we could have done to bring him down. And that's half the problem here now." He paused. "We don't have a solution for Super-Normals other than trying to live at peace with them. Not everyone is equal parts powerful, beautiful, and peace-loving like Blurr over there."

Blurr's cheeks flushed red as she glanced over at Paladin. "Thank you, Colonel."

"We're flattered by your presence here, Colonel, but I'm sure you

49

didn't come to New Chicago to thank us in person. We already received a medal of commendation in the mail," Paladin said.

"Indeed, Paladin," Matheson answered. "The United States wants to change the way Super-Normals are viewed on a global scale. Our relations and coexistence are hinged on our ability to break through ignorance. Normals need to know that Super-Normals are here to serve a greater purpose than just fetching cats from trees and rescuing women from burning buildings. They have to know that you and others like you have their...I mean to say, *our* backs. We don't need another war we can't win."

"So what are you asking, Colonel?" Lydia asked.

"I want you all to take the reins of a global defense force initiative we are in the preliminary stages of creating. It will serve as the first line of defense of whatever threats may exist beyond the boundaries of our ozone layer," Matheson said.

"*May* exist, Colonel?" Paladin asked. "Sounds like you may know more than you're letting on."

Colonel Matheson looked down at his hat as he folded it over a couple of times in his hands. "There's nothing definitive yet, son, but...call it a hunch. We just want to know if we can depend on you *if* it becomes necessary."

"You have our support, Colonel," Paladin said.

"Good. Others like you...Super-Normals. Can you recruit them to the cause?" Matheson asked.

"I know a guy," Blurr chimed. "I'm sure there are a few more we can rally to our cause."

Paladin clenched his teeth, and Lydia snickered from across the table.

"The Majesties? Ex-military…They'd be a welcome addition. But I'm afraid our Intel says that they're not available," Colonel Matheson said.

"They got something better to do than save the planet?" Blurr asked.

"Possibly. Reports say they're no longer *on* the planet," Colonel Matheson said.

"Oh. Well, okay then," Blurr said.

"I think we can handle it, Colonel," Paladin said.

"Son, we will need all the help you can get. Weren't there three of you? Where's the other fellow? The one who was on trial?" Colonel Matheson asked, looking around.

"He's—" Blurr started, but Paladin cut in.

"On a special recon mission. We're holding things down in his stead. When will this initiative be ready?" Paladin asked, quickly trying to steer the conversation in another direction.

"No time soon. Maybe in the next six months to a year. But in the meantime, if there are any more talented folks like you here in New Chicago, it'd be best to reach out. The more, the merrier. What we'll do on our end until then is to put out public service announcements to soften up the world's perspective of Super-Normals. It's what we call our F.R.I.E.N.D.S. campaign. Future Readiness Involves Every

Necessary Dedicated Source. Hopefully, once people understand our future involves a collaborative effort, then we'll have forward movement."

"*Hopefully*, Colonel?" Blurr asked, sounding unconvinced.

Colonel Matheson stood and motioned his soldiers to the door. "We've taken up much of your time. Again, we appreciate everything you're doing here. Crime in Chicago is down to an all-time low. Which is—b"

"Better than it's been, but there's still a ways to go," Paladin said, standing too.

"What can we do to help?" Colonel Matheson asked.

"We need resources, Colonel," Paladin said. "The city is spent and can't continue to rely solely on sponsors. We need to take Hero City's financial support arms outside of the state. The feds need to start pitching in."

"We hear you, son. Put something together for me to present to the House and Senate. You've got their attention," Matheson said as he handed Paladin his card. "We'll be in touch soon."

Paladin offered to shake the Colonel's hand. "Thank you."

The Colonel held his place. "No offense, son, but I'm not too big on pleasantries."

One of the soldiers approached Blurr from the side. "I, on the other hand, don't mind a little contact at all," he said, staring at her.

"Stay in your place, soldier," Colonel Matheson barked. The soldier maintained his position as if ignoring anything Colonel Matheson said.

"I said, hold your place, soldier! That's an order," he repeated, this time at a tone twice the level as before.

As if waking from a trance, the soldier shook his head and bowed. "I'm sorry," he said, just before backing away and heading to the front door.

"Sorry about that, ma'am," Colonel Matheson said.

"No problem," Blurr replied.

The colonel placed his hat on his head and tipped it at the ladies before turning to exit. Once the door closed, B.R.A.I.N. spoke.

"I was analyzing the Colonel's vital signs, pupil size, and sweat glands while he was talking. The varying oscillations were all over the place. Although the majority of what he said was true, he was definitely hiding something. That last outburst was very unexpected."

"Soldier boys are always a little crazy for beautiful women. I didn't take offense," Blurr said.

"Still, they were a peculiar bunch indeed."

Paladin looked down at the card the Colonel left him. "Yeah, I agree. Peculiar *indeed*."

ACT II

"I urge the citizens of New Chicago to reach out to your fellow citizens, Super-Normals and Capes, more specifically, to get out and vote for new, fair registration laws and referendums. We cannot continue to live in the age of separatism and hatred for our fellow human beings, no matter how different they are. If we can't live in harmony with one another, mankind's continued evolution to something greater will be stunted, leaving all of us vulnerable for attacks, both foreign and domestic."

Mayor Corella, year 2036 – World Summit Speech of Unity at DePaul University

Chapter 5
The artifact

Sebastian left the girls downstairs and quickly raced into the lab's storage container housing the S3.1. He folded his arms and stared at the suit as tiny robot hands circled it, making small repairs along the torso, arms, and legs. Sparks ignited at the tips of the tools fastened to the pincers of metal fingers. Along the outside of the glass, a green 3D projection of vital information concerning the condition of the repairs and upgrades flashed by, refreshing every ten to fifteen seconds.

"Eighty-four percent, huh?" Karla asked from behind, starling him.

But Sebastian kept looking forward. "Yeah. Shouldn't be long now."

"It really kicked butt out there. It wasn't even at full strength. Imagine what it can really do next time."

"Yeah...imagine."

"The people of New Chicago will be screaming your name. But it's less about the suit and more about the man inside that really counts."

"Really? He's just doing what he can to help everyone," Sebastian answered dryly.

"Hero City is safe again, and it's all because of you," Karla said.

Sebastian remained silent, mulling over a few thousand choice words he'd like to share with her. Frustration filled his veins, and he didn't know how to tell her.

Karla touched his shoulder gently. "You okay?"

Sebastian leaned away and turned to see her. "Of course, I'm not okay. Sometimes I don't know what we're doing here."

"What do you mean *what we're doing here?*" I thought we were saving the city."

"We...the team of heroes are saving the city. But we—meaning me and you—I don't always know where we stand."

"Sebas, I...things are always complicated with a gal like me. I've got a lot of baggage, and I can't always be depended upon to make just decisions. I'm...erratic at best. I thought you knew that when you signed on."

"I can handle erratic. We all are from time to time. It's just that I don't like not always knowing if I'm number one. You're always number one with me. Always have been. Ever since I laid eyes on you back in school."

Karla sighed. "Oh, Sebas. My past is never just in the past. You're such a clean, perfect guy. I sometimes feel a little odd—guilty even—for trying to even embrace the idea of having you all to myself."

"But it doesn't have to be that way. Keep the past where it belongs. Let me help you."

"I'd like to. Really, I would. But I don't know how."

Sebastian took her hands and squeezed them. "You can start by opening up to me. Talk to me, Karla. Let me know what's in that beautiful head of yours. We lost touch all these years since school and I want, I mean, *need* to know what happened during that time."

Karl remained silent and simply nodded.

"Can you do that, for us?" Sebastian asked.

"I can," she whispered. "I mean…I will."

Sebastian moved closer and planted a long, soft kiss on her lips, squeezing her body with his arms. He felt Karla's hand slide along his muscular frame, up from his waist until finally pausing at the base of his head, firmly rubbing his neck.

"Get a room," Lydia said, interrupting their kissing session.

Sebastian rolled his eyes and looked over at her, her frame filling the doorway. "We are in a room."

Lydia walked over, holding a tablet. "Well, I'm here now. So cut it out." She held the tablet out to Karla. "Looks like your mob buddies finally slipped up. The E.I.Es have picked up their scent. It appears that one of them picked up on a private conversation between a few hoodlums and followed them to an old abandoned warehouse on Fifth and Lenox."

"Isn't that the old storage facility for the city circus?" Sabastian asked.

"Yep. Looks like the clowns are returning," Karla said, handing the tablet back to Lydia.

Lydia took it and starting pecking on the screen. "Something big is going down tonight. And you all should get moving ASAP." She flashed them the screen. Numbers began to tick down. "B.R.A.I.N. estimates about two to four hours from now, all—and I mean *all*—the mob bosses and buddies will be migrating there."

"And they didn't include me," Sebastian said in a low sarcastic tone.

"Looks like a big round-up is at stake," Lydia said.

Sebastian looked over at the glass casing housing the S3.1. "Ninety-five percent. Almost ready."

The case opened and the S3.1 slid forward, hanging from metal clamps. "Oh, just take the darn thing out and get going," B.R.A.I.N. said. "Five percent isn't going to make you any faster. All three variants are fully functional. Just press the breastplate in the middle and the HUD in your helmet will let you know which one is active."

"Sweet," Sebastian said. He took the S3.1 from the clamps and held it up. "You sure I don't need the last five?"

"Get going," Lydia and B.R.A.I.N. said simultaneously.

"I'm out," Sebastian said.

***

Moments later, Blurr and Paladin found themselves standing atop the old Sears building, looking over the formerly abandoned warehouse.

"Not abandoned anymore," Karla whispered, eyeing the situation from a pair of seer-scope binoculars. She pulled them away from her eyes and handed them to Paladin.

Paladin gave a look. "Wow! B.R.A.I.N. wasn't lying. They're packing them in by the droves."

"I know this doesn't sound anything like me, but maybe we should call in police backup."

"No," Paladin barked. "We can do this by ourselves. The police haven't helped us a lick in the past few months. They didn't kill Caine, and they certainly didn't help solve that murder. They held Thief captive. Remember?"

"Yeah, but I just thought that—"

"No, Karla. I got this," Paladin said bluntly. "I mean, *we* got this."

"Fine. What's the play, then?"

Sebastian pulled the seer-scope down. "I sent a couple of E.I.Es in to do some close-up surveillance. We'll wait until all of them are inside. Then we make our move."

Blurr turned away and took a seat along the ledge of the Sears building, dangling her feet over the edge. She crossed her legs and stared off into the distance. "Good. Then wait it is."

Paladin felt a chill run between them. "Look, I'm sorry I snapped at you. I didn't mean to."

"It's okay. I get it. You're just as anxious as I am. We'll take these punks out. No sweat."

"Look, back there at the house, when the Colonel asked about help. He thought you were referencing the Majesties, but you were talking about Thief, weren't you?"

"Yes, I was."

"You still share something between you two, don't you?"

"Yes, but not like that. Not like you think. Thief and I are…at least *were*, one and the same; two peas in a pod. It's hard to shake that type of bond."

"What bond? Being some man's side piece isn't what I call having a connection."

"He had a wife, yes. But he wasn't in love with her. He had kids…a family. But he wasn't dedicated to them. Not like he should have been. He made me believe I was a priority."

"But it was a lie, Karla."

"Don't you think I know that?" Blurr yelled. "I…I…I wanted to believe otherwise. He got into me." She pointed at her heart. "Not here," then pointed at her head. "But *here*."

"I get it. I don't understand, but I get it."

"How could you? You don't share the same darkness that Thief and I do. We were runners."

"Runners from what?"

Blurr stood from the ledge and walked toward him. "The truth. The truth of who we really were. A couple of outcasts. Losers."

Paladin cupped her shoulders. "You're not a loser, Karla. I love you. And that should let you know how important you are to me. To the world."

Blurr smiled lightly. "Thank you."

"I know we're chasing down these mob bosses because they deserve a good whipping for what they've done to this city. But what else is at stake? Be real with me. What are you looking for?"

Blurr's eyes widened. "I—"

Just as she was about to speak, one of the E.I.Es flashed into their periphery, buzzing. "Guys," Lydia's voice boomed from it. "They're all inside. And the main leader, Titan, is there with them."

"Uh, who's Titan?" Paladin asked.

"We're close," Blurr whispered. "This is it."

"What's it?" Paladin asked. His grasp on her shoulder tightened.

Blurr looked at him. "No time to explain. We bust them up and call the cops to do the cleanup." She tried to pull away, but Paladin held her still, his strength variant already activated.

"After that, you tell me everything. The secrets end here. Tonight, Karla."

"Agreed," Blurr said. She disappeared from his hands in an instant and stood along the edge of the building. "Get the speed variant up and running. We need to hurry."

Something in the back of Paladin's mind pulled at him, tugging so hard that he was compelled to follow after her despite his better judgment. But it wasn't love this time. Not that thing that drove him to unabatedly chase after her former Super-Normal self as Cheetah-Girl. No, this was something else altogether.

It was fear.

The thought stabbed at him. The idea of somehow losing Karla—the girl he'd willingly sacrifice the entire fate of the city for—sent a wave of adrenaline pulsing through his veins, egging him into a frenzy of wild feet as he launched from his stance and sped along the side of the building in pursuit of both Blurr and her rebellious nature. Why she was so desperate to fight an army of thugs and their mysterious leader didn't matter anymore. All that mattered was that she was safe.

When Paladin finally came to a halt inside the warehouse, the realization that he'd passed Blurr and slammed his shoulder into the front doors—bending them back on their hinges like two broken tongue depressors—was only upstaged by the follow-up entrance of his female counterpart.

Blurr flashed his periphery and swirled around the room twice, separating about two dozen goons from their assault rifles and releasing their clips before they could blink twice. The sound of the ammunition clanging the floor was refreshing. Paladin made a sweeping gaze of their surroundings. The three-story room was a perfect square, with armed mob soldiers littered across each level. With the stairs along the corners as the only means of safe passage, it was time to move fast.

Shots rang out speedily fashion as expected, but not a single round was successful in hitting two Super-Normal speedsters. Paladin and Blurr made their way through the layer of goons, flattening them like pancakes and placing well-timed punches and kicks as they raced along. With some luck, bullets meant to hit them found new homes within the flesh of unwary assailants. Blood and screams laced the night air, along with the floors and walls.

By the time Paladin and Blurr circled the first two floors and arrived on the third, Titan greeted them, front and center. Paladin and Blurr came to a stop just short of him. An opening in the roof welcomed the cool Chicago breeze.

"Stop!" Titan screamed with an extended arm.

He was what Paladin would expect the mob boss leader to look like. He was abnormally tall, possibly somewhere between seven to eight feet, with massive arms and legs that would have put The Rock to shame. He wore a silver, tight-fitted, long-sleeved bodysuit top with stretched blue jean pants and brown ankle-high boots. His opposite hand was fisted around a long knife whose blade shimmered in the moonlight. The red bandana topping his head reminded Paladin of an ancient Aztec warrior.

"You dare invade my territory tonight? This is sacred ground," Titan said.

"Good, I was wondering if you had the goods," Blurr said.

"Goods?" Paladin asked in her direction.

Blurr ignored his conjecture and continued to partake in a private conversation with the oversized chieftain.

"We're not here to kill you…technically. Just to collect what you have. What you've stolen. Property of a friend of mine," Blurr said, pointing a finger.

Titan laughed, tossing the hilt of his knife around in his hand. "You have some nerve, whore. Nothing here belongs to anyone but me." He smiled widely. "And, yes, I've heard about you. You're just a toy for men. But I am not without manly needs myself. Once I cut you, I'll play a little as well. It'll be gruesome, but doing it the basic way nowadays is well…boring."

Paladin screamed aloud and engaged Titan head-on, his strength variant now active, sacrificing speed for power. Titan seemed to anticipate the move, dropping back into a defensive position with his knife drawn back in hand by his off leg and his left arm guarding his body like a shield. As Paladin threw a punch in Titan's direction, he parred with a block and swing of his knife.

The knife found its way into Paladin's thigh plating, but not before it doubled in thickness, swallowing the tip of the blade. Intuitively, Paladin had increased the strength gauge of the suit, which made him larger and stronger. Paladin swung a second time and connected with Titan's jaw, but the giant didn't even flinch. Paladin felt a wave of heat pulse through his hand, and into his wrist, arm, and shoulder. The pain knocked him to one knee.

Titan smiled. "My turn." He grabbed Paladin by the head and lifted him from the floor with ease, making the hulking hero look more like a helpless ragdoll. Blurr swooped in from behind and, just as she was about to attack, Titan slid to the side and backslapped her with his other hand, sending her sprawling across the floor and into the opposite wall with a thud.

Blurr crawled to her side. "What," she whispered in disbelief.

Titan slammed Paladin into the floor multiple times, loosening the wooden floorboards before finally pulling his knife free from Paladin's armor and extending the blade overhead. "This is mine. This city is mine. And your souls are mine."

The large knife began to glow, and Titan's eyes blazed indigo blue. He began to chant something foreign to both Paladin and Blurr, reminiscent of some ancient Indian warrior. Titan plunged the knife into Paladin's chest, piercing the breastplate just inches from his flesh. Paladin responded, grabbing Titan's arm with both hands as he strained to stop Titan's blade from advancing any farther.

"Sebastian," Paladin heard Lydia cry over the comms.

"You will be a perfect sacrifice for The Coming," Titan said, a strain in his voice.

Blurr dashed in again, locking her arms around Titan's neck. Her arms vibrated at incredible speed, quickly closing off his windpipe. Titan dropped Paladin to the ground and grabbed Blurr's arms, struggling to pry them loose. He tumbled backward and rammed Blurr into the wall behind them. His gigantic hand gripped both of Blurr's arms. He freed the other hand and began to send wave after wave of elbow thrusts into Blurr's side.

Paladin grabbed the hilt of the knife in his chest and eyed the scene across from him. He could see Blurr losing her strength as each elbow collided with her torso. He had to act fast.

The S3.1 had been damaged and wilted to half the size it had been only moments ago, compliments of the well-placed knife blade.

"Try speed," Lydia said.

"I can't. I'm stuck in the strength phase," he replied.

As Blurr finally tumbled to the floor, Titan turned and stood over her. "No, I will punish you," he said, raising his fist overhead.

Paladin snatched the knife free and tossed it at Titan with every ounce of strength she could muster. But it was enough. The blade tore into Titan from behind and split through his chest in the front, lodging into the wall some ten feet away. Titan turned to Paladin, holding the gaping hole in his gargantuan frame. Rage filled his eyes.

Titan charged at Paladin furiously with blinding speed that rivaled Blurr's. Before Paladin could react, Titan was upon him, digging his fingers into the protective exoskeleton of the S3.1. He began to rip off layers of armor like some ravenous beast, and Paladin did his best to fend off his advances with punches and elbows to Titan's face that did nothing to slow him down. And although blood drained from Titan at an impressive rate, it seemed to do nothing to weaken his resolve. If Paladin had to guess, he seemed even...stronger.

"Sebastian, Titan is growing stronger. Like he summoned some kind of rage modifier," Lydia yelled.

"This isn't Dungeons and Dragons, Lydia," Paladin returned, just as the center of the S3.1 fileted open exposing Sebastian to the cool Chicago night.

"Probably could have used that five percent, B.R.A.I.N.," Paladin said.

Titan leaned in closer and peered into the eye sockets of the S3.1 as if he could see into Sebastian's mind. "I said...your soul is mine," he hissed.

Titan reeled back, and Paladin flinched in anticipation of the final death-blow. But, before he could deliver, Titan burst into an explosion of ash, dropping Paladin to the floor. When the dust settled, only Blurr remained, her entire body vibrating in a translucent state.

"Karla," Paladin cried, his hands covering his face.

Blurr raised her hands to her face and stared as if she was watching the sunrise for the first time. "Sebastian, what's happening to me?"

Paladin stood and ran toward Blurr, somewhat afraid to make contact, but more fearful not to. He passed on sound judgment and reached out for her wrists, attempting to charge the strength module as strong as possible. To Paladin's surprise, he struck gold, wrapping his fingers around solid skin. Blurr's body slowly solidified once more. Paladin couldn't resist wrapping his arms around her entire body.

"I'm detecting high amounts of radiation emanating from Blurr, Sebastian," B.R.A.I.N. said over the comms. "You're being exposed."

Paladin didn't care. He was exasperated by the proximity of both his and her near-death experiences.

"Sebastian, you guys need to get out of there, quickly. More soldiers are closing in on your position. You're exposed," Lydia warned.

The words awoke Paladin from his despondency. "Can you run, Karla?" he whispered, gazing into her eyes.

Blurr nodded. "Yes," she replied faintly.

Paladin took her by the hand and began to make a run for the window but noticed that Blurr had pulled away, running in the opposite direction. "Blurr," he cried.

Blurr dashed for the blade and dislodged it from the wall. As the remaining soldiers spilled into the room and trained their guns on the two of them, Blurr burst into full gear, snatched Paladin by the wrist, and bolted the two of them out the window.

Chapter 6
Deep space

Lydia allows herself a moment to cry heavy tears as Sebastian and Karla settled in beside her on the couch. After entering the penthouse through the roof entrance, Sebastian had tossed what remained of the S3.1 onto the floor in disgust and stripped down to his black spandex bottoms. Karla still wore her baby blue leotard, which showed minor wear and tear from the night's fray. Her gold cape had taken the brunt of the fight, as a long slash ran down the middle.

She'd already freed herself from the hoody attachment and allowed her long, dark, curly hair a chance to breathe. Her goggles were cracked in the left eye socket and a dark bruise underneath her eye had already started to fade from her accelerated healing powers. But Sebastian wasn't so lucky, no doubt earning a few cracked ribs.

He considered himself lucky to have not broken a leg from the thrashing he absorbed from Titan. Fatigued by the constant flow of Lydia's tears and the dreary silence of the room, he could restrain his questions no longer.

"What happened back there?" he asked, staring at Karla.

"What do you mean?" she replied.

"I mean that ass whipping we just took. I mean that knife over there on the kitchen counter. I mean that evil Super-Normal mob boss. I mean the entire dismal night. That's what I *mean*!" Sebastian stood as he emphasized the last word of his rant.

Karla remained seated and met his gaze with a calmness that kept his blood boiling.

Lydia sucked up her tears and reached out for him. "Sebas, wait a minute. Maybe Karla doesn't know—"

"No, I have answers, Lydia," Karla said, standing now as well. She walked over to the kitchen counter and picked up the knife, eyeing it in the gleam of the recessed lighting. "This knife is an artifact of ancient lore. Or, well, of future tech. I'm not quite sure yet."

"Not quite sure? You've been having us risk our lives over the past few weeks to hunt down mob bosses and goons for an artifact that you're not even sure about?" Sebastian asked, disgusted.

"Well, I've only been fed limited information about it and was honestly operating a little blindly, hanging mainly on the word of a good friend," Karla said.

"Who, Slaycick?" Sebastian asked.

"No…Thief," Karla replied.

"Thief!" Sebastian hissed. "Oh, man. You've got to be kidding me, right? Please say you're kidding me?"

Karla placed the knife on the counter and folded her arms, staring at Sebastian with a slight head tilt. "No, I'm not kidding. Thief knows what he's talking about. I trust him."

Sebastian stepped from around the couch and closed the distance between them. "You what? After what he pulled on you? After he treated you like some—"

"Don't say anything you might regret, Sebastian," Lydia warned, now standing too.

"Oh no. Let him say it. Go ahead, spit it out. I know you're ashamed of me. I know you hate my past. It's written all over your face, and you just bubble over with rage when anyone brings it up," Karla said.

Sebastian paused. Karla was right. The surge of adrenaline flowing through his veins at that moment was the same as what he felt when anyone spoke of Karla's past—especially the freshness of the recent experience with Titan. But it didn't come from a place of shame as much as it originated from a place of chivalry. In some crazy, unexplainable way, he felt obligated to fight for her dignity, to salvage any piece of her purity, even if it had been given away. But how could he tell her that without making her feel any less self-conscious? Instead of responding, he took the easy way out.

"You're right. I'm sorry. I am ashamed," he said softly.

Karla's eyes dropped to the floor. "I knew it."

"He didn't mean that," Lydia said in a failed attempt to soften the blow.

Karla raised a hand. "Don't, Lydia. I don't need a Band-Aid. Those wounds close quickly and I move on. Always have."

"Karla, I didn't mean it that way. I just hate what they say about you. It kills me to think that they know the real you," Sebastian said.

"You don't get it, Sebastian," Karla said, her eyes not meeting his. "Maybe that's all I am. Maybe that *is* the real me."

BRAXTON A. COSBY

"No! You are an angel and you are priceless in my eyes. We all have flaws and imperfections. No one is perfect. And I refuse to let *you* or anyone say anything about you to the contrary." He could see the tears welling up in her eyes. It jerked at his heartstrings. But he couldn't let the pain of seeing her shaken throw him off course. He had to have answers. "What about Titan? Who is he?"

"More like *what* was he," Karla replied. "Categorically, he was a Super-Normal. But not like one from Earth. Not like the ones from the Storm. Supposedly, he came from the stars."

"Eww, like our alien friend Menzuo?" Lydia asked with a smile.

"Like him," Karla answered. "When Thief left to try to figure out the mysteries of those spores we found on Caine's ashes after the fight, he had been corresponding with me through email, giving me updates from his contacts in the Middle East. Apparently, he'd made contact with the Majesties and they led him to a person of interest who kept a dossier on alien Super-Normals. Thief, being Thief, came across the dossier and confiscated the Intel. All he shared with me is that there was a crime boss with a special skillset who was roaming through New Chicago carrying an artifact of high importance. Asked me if I could lift it off of him and that he'd be heading back to this side of the world soon. Said he'd be in touch when he did."

Sebastian folded his arms across his chest. "So the artifact, huh? That's all he wanted?"

"I don't know. Why don't you ask him yourself?" Karla said.

Sebastian followed her eyes as they hovered over his right shoulder.

"He's behind me, isn't he?"

Karla nodded.

Sebastian turned to find Thief floating just a few feet in the air, fading in and out of focus similarly to that of Zenith when he passes through walls. Thief dropped on the tile floor and solidified. "Hey there, everyone. I saw Zenith on the way over and took a small dose of his powers before I made it in. Thought it'd make for quite a dramatic entrance. Pulled it off, don't you think?" Thief asked, focusing on Lydia.

"I'd say so. Pretty cool," Lydia said.

"How'd you manage to keep it this long? I thought you could only steal powers when people were within one hundred feet?" Karla asked.

"Been learning to perfect that minor limitation in my abilities. Learned a lot across seas," Thief said with a smirk. "How've you been, Karla?"

"Perfect," Karla snapped.

"What brings you all this way? Finally," Sebastian said.

"Well, from what I just heard, it looks like you had a question for me," Thief said.

Sebastian's hands fisted at his side. "Oh, I've got a *lot* of questions."

"Well, you might want to grab one of those fancy suits for that sort of meeting, bloke," Thief said. "Your current situation is more *casual* than business. Don't want to impose on your busy schedule, *rich boy*."

"Oh, I'm sure I can pencil you in for a closed-door meeting," Sebastian said.

"Cockfight," Lydia said.

"Stop it, right now," Karla said. "We don't have time for this crap."

Thief brushed past Sebastian, walked over to Karla and gave her a big hug. "You sure you doing okay, gorgeous?"

"I'm fine," Karla replied.

"What's that bruise under your eye?" Thief asked.

"It was nothing," Karla replied.

"Oh, yeah, nothing. Just something she picked up from a super-freak alien, Super-Normal mob boss that you sent us to full force into without any warning," Sebastian said.

Thief wore a look of confusion. "Titan?"

"The one and deadly," Sebastian said.

"You were supposed to wait," Thief said, watching Karla intently.

"I did wait. But he was only in town for a while, and I didn't want him to get away," Karla said.

"I intentionally asked you not to engage him if you could. He is super dangerous," Thief said.

"*Was* super dangerous," Sebastian said.

Thief's eyes widened. "He's dead, Cherie?" he asked, looking at Karla. When she nodded, he turned to Sebastian and pointed. "You killed him?"

"Uh, no, not exactly. I weakened him a bit though," Sebastian said.

"And then I finished him off," Karla said.

"You should have seen her. Did some kinda wicked vibration thingy and took him out. Incineration station," Lydia said.

"Inciner–what?" Thief asked.

"I still don't know what I did," Karla said. "He was about to kill Sebastian and I freaked. I jumped to my feet, closed in from behind, and all I could remember was this deep heat generating in my body from the soles of my feet to the top of my head. Even my hair follicles felt hot. Before I knew it, every inch of my body was moving at supersonic speed. I could barely see my own hands in front of my face. On instinct alone, I slammed my fists into Titan's back and just like that—poof—he was gone."

Thief cupped his chin. "Interesting. Tell me more. Did he turn into ashes?"

"Yep, a blaze of glory," Sebastian said.

"Did you get a sample?" Thief asked.

Sebastian swallowed hard. "No."

"No? Come on, we really could have used that Intel," Thief said.

Embarrassed, Sebastian attempted to recover. "Well, how did you expect us to think of something like that at *that* moment? You're the super sleuth, not us. We just killed some super baddie and a horde of goons were bearing down on us."

"This is true," Thief said sarcastically.

Sebastian grunted. "Please."

Karla reached toward the kitchen counter and picked up the knife. "We did manage to grab this." She handed it over to Thief.

"Wow. So you did retrieve it. This means everything," Thief said.

"Um, means what?" Sebastian asked.

"The dossier I was able to *borrow* from a target outlined a rare artifact that linked not one, but two species of creatures from different worlds. Humans from Earth and Rothandians from somewhere in deep space. A place well beyond our research, hidden in the dark matter," Thief explained, flipping the knife over twice in his hand. "It said that the Rothandians and humans both shared the same origin from a higher being, but that the Rothandians had progressed much faster than humanity because of their obedience to God. They were rewarded. They found out about the existence of humans through their research and became incensed with destroying them because they considered them inferior due to their ignorance of higher evolution. Not from just a technological side but a spiritual one as well. They vowed to wipe out humanity one day."

"So what, they sent a knife as a warning?" Sebastian asked, trying to understand.

"No. It is thought that a traveler came to Earth several hundreds of years ago to warn us of what was to come. His name was Apagos. He was what they referred to as Palatmos or high priest. He didn't share the same sentiments as his fellow Rothandians and theorized that God would not want any of his children to perish, and to think of destroying any of them just because of their lack of obedience was sacrilegious. He was thought of as a heretic…an outcast."

"So he left, came here to warn us, and then what?" Lydia asked.

Thief smirked. "He died. Apparently the pollutants on this planet were too much for him. But before he passed away, he gave his hunting knife to a great Indian Chieftain name Solaris. It possessed great powers. It was thought to have been enchanted by him before his passing. Further research over the years revealed that it too had been laced with spores. Dark Spores. The same ones on the remains of Caine."

"Wait a minute. So now we aren't just up against Super-Normals on Earth, but alien ones as well," Sebastian said.

"Possibly. The dossier didn't give any dates or times of when a possible invasion would be coming, but I feel that the threat is imminent," Thief said.

"Titan said some mumbo-jumbo about taking our souls. Know what he could've meant?" Karla asked.

"Titan was a descendant of Solaris. If he followed the traditions of his ancestors, he believed that he was some mythical warrior that could steal the souls of his enemies and get stronger," Thief said.

"Colonel Matheson said that he was interested in putting together a team to defend the planet from an alien invasion. Maybe the United States already knows something about movement up in space," Sebastian said.

"They approached you?" Thief asked, surprised.

"Yeah. Tried to recruit us all. Even asked about you," Sebastian said.

"Then we are running out of precious time," Thief said.

Lydia stepped forward and extended her hand. "What can we do?"

"What can *you* do?" Thief asked.

"I was being polite. Give me the damn knife. I know what to do. B.R.A.I.N. and I will get on analyzing this thing and figure out what clues it can give us about these Dark Spores." Lydia smiled and rubbed her hands together. "I feel so good having a name for them now. So connected to the purpose."

Thief raised an eyebrow Karla's way. "Don't worry, Lydia's harmless. She's just a super bad-ass geek with an obsession with figuring things out."

Thief handed it to Lydia, who immediately bolted upstairs, talking some gibberish about quantum physics that even Sebastian couldn't make sense of.

"What about Karla? What do you think happened to her?" Sebastian asked.

"I'm not entirely sure," Thief said, giving her a quick once-over. "Whispers among other Super-Normals is that there is some link between emotions and elevating superpowers to another level. Somehow, maybe she tapped into that space when she felt fear."

"It wasn't fear," Karla chimed.

"Then what was it?" Thief asked.

Karla shook her head and walked off. "I need to take a nap." She gave a quick speed burst and climbed the stairs in no time before anyone else could ask any more questions, leaving Thief and Sebastian alone.

"Listen, Sebastian, I'm worried about Karla," Thief said.

"Oh, really? Now you're worried?"

'Seriously, I didn't send her to get that artifact. She did that on her own. I meant for her to find out if Titan had it and to wait before engaging."

"Then why did she do it?"

"I don't know. She can be a bit erratic at times. Unpredictable."

"Tell me about it."

"We have to keep an eye on her."

"Why keep this just between you and her all this time? I didn't hear a peep from you since you left."

Thief sighed. "I needed to go silent. I was deep underground over there. If I contacted too many people, my cover may have been blown. I was using a decryption tech that allowed me to reach out to only one person with short burst emails. They would last for mere microseconds. One send, one read. Only Karla had the skillset to read them before they would self-destruct. No hard feelings, mate."

"I get it."

Thief looked around, eying the penthouse with slight admiration. "Nice squat, Sebastian."

"Thanks. We get by," Sebastian said with an air of arrogance.

Thief looked around the room. "Things have certainly changed since I left. What happened to all the endorsement deals?"

"The ones we had when you left are still there, but the focus isn't on gaining new ones anymore. People just want to see what we do, not hear it."

"Theatricality has gone mundane now, huh?"

Sebastian shrugged. "I guess so."

"Another thing is tugging at my mind."

"Shoot."

"Tell me, why haven't you all moved into The Beacon yet? It's supposed to be your headquarters now, right?"

"Yeah, it's supposed to be. But after we killed Caine, Mystikal and Mirage went ghost. We couldn't assume that The Beacon was safe. It had to be compromised in some way. We could stay, but with Lydia working with us now full-time, it'd expose her. She's only a Normal."

Thief chuckled. "Ha."

"What's so funny about that?"

"Look at you. Aren't you the *Super-Normal* all of a sudden," Thief said, making small air quotes with his fingers when he said Super-Normal.

"I'm just as much of a hero as any of you."

Thief stepped in close, nose-to-nose with Sebastian. "Don't get things twisted, mate. You may be with us, but you ain't one of us."

"I've got ten thousand that I can make you eat those words in less than two rounds."

"Is that why it's in the shop for repairs? That suit ain't as super as you think."

"Funny, I don't recall being the one strapped to a column in the bowels of New Chicago. Tell me, how's the smell down there? I heard that nothing wakes you up more than the aroma of fresh feces."

Thief gnashed his teeth and raised a fist at him. "You better be glad she likes you."

"Check that...*Loves* me," Sebastian said.

Thief smiled and lowered his fist. "You rich kids are all alike, thinking that money can buy you everything. You may be close, but you'll never be *connected*. Not like I was...with her."

Sebastian swung as hard as he could, taking direct aim at Thief's jaw. Just as his fist was mere inches away from his face, Thief phased out of focus, sending Sebastian whirling around from the momentum of his swing. He tumbled to the floor as he lost his balance. He glared over his shoulder at Thief, and Thief held out a cautionary hand at Sebastian. "Hey, hey, hey. Whoa! I'm sorry, mate. I can see that you really like Karla. My bad." Thief offered Sebastian a hand and helped him to his feet. "I was just pulling your chain to see where you really stand. You've got heart. She needs that."

"Why do you care so much about her? You couldn't. You had a wife...a family. This *thing* you had with Karla was just a game. If you couldn't love the woman who bore your children, then how the hell could you truly care for some sexual pastime?"

"It wasn't like that at all," Thief said with a sigh. He paused and looked down at his feet as if pondering a more appropriate answer to Sebastian's question. "You truly wouldn't understand even if I told you, *rich kid.*"

"I wasn't always rich, you know. I earned my position."

"Yeah, I know. Read your dossier too during my downtime across seas. Your Uncle Rooney jumpstarted all your hard work."

"He may have given me the tools, but I had to put in the work. *Nobody* gave me anything."

Thief nodded. "I know. Just tugging that chain again. A little war of words." Thief held out his hand. "Let's call it a truce for now. Dig?"

Sebastian looked down at Thief's open hand and took it, halfway expecting Thief to phase out again as some childish joke. He gave it a firm squeeze. "We've got bigger fish to fry."

Thief squeezed back, just as firm. "Agreed. Tell me more about the Colonel."

"Well, he and his men approached us the other night and spilled the beans on quite a lot of goings-on. Apparently, there's some new project in the works that the United States is interested in recruiting us for. Part of some F.R.I.E.N.D.S. initiative. You included."

"I've got enough *friends,* and I've never been one for team sports."

"What friends?"

"The kind that traipses sewers for you in their spare time."

Sebastian smiled. It was the first time Thief had referred to him and Cheetah-Girl's daring rescue. And although it was a terrible attempt at anything remotely to a *thank you*, he figured it was the best he was going to get. "As far as solo opportunities go, I'm not really sure there's any room for freelancing. Colonel Matheson seemed quite concerned about convincing us to get on board."

"Did he give a timeline?"

"Nah," Sebastian said. He snapped his finger. "Oh, but he offered up something else. This group or team is supposed to be part of a global defense force he says is designed to protect the planet from threats outside our ozone layer. When I drilled him for more details, he was very vague, only saying it was more of a hunch."

"The United States has a bad history of non-successful *hunches*."

"Right."

Thief stroked his chin. "Hmm. But I must admit, I'm a little more than intrigued by all this. The timing of the artifact and the sudden concern of worldly threats can't all be just coincidence."

"What are you thinking?"

"I'm thinking that the Colonel owes us a few more answers. What kind of timeline do you have on getting that suit of yours operational?"

"B.R.A.I.N.?" Sebastian asked aloud.

"I've been working on a couple of new composites already," B.R.A.I.N. said.

"Composites? Who greenlit that?" Sebastian asked.

"No one," B.R.A.I.N. replied, sounding somewhat annoyed. "I figured it'd be nice to have a few on hand to subvert all of the downtimes of repairs. No Super-Normal can afford to be on the sideline. Put me in, coach."

"Karla told me about your *boyfriend*," Thief said. "Quite the piece of tech. I like him."

"I'm not Sebastian's boyfriend. He's not my type," B.R.A.I.N. said.

"Too ugly," Thief joked.

"No, too *pretty*," B.R.A.I.N. said.

"Ahh, ha. My dog," Sebastian chimed. "So when will they be

ready?"

"One just finalized two minutes ago. Are you planning to take it for a spin?" B.R.A.I.N. asked.

Sebastian gave Thief a side-eye. Thief winked back. "I'd say it's only prudent to test all tech before giving it a full go. What do you say, Thief, think you can keep up?"

Thief inhaled deeply, closing his eyes while balling his fists. After a couple of seconds, he opened them again, meeting Sebastian's. "Yep. Just took a little drag of Karla's speed. No offense, bro."

Sebastian smirked. "None taken."

***

The night air was brisk, carrying a slight chill that slipped through the tiniest slits of the S3.1's seemingly impenetrable exoskeleton. Sebastian felt every bit of it as he and Thief sped across numerous city blocks until coming to a stop just on the outskirts of a local military outpost. The ten-foot-high barbed-wire fence was just enough to encourage a moment of game planning.

The hope was that somehow Colonel Matheson hadn't yet left the sanctuary of New Chicago for Washington D.C. If there was an outside chance of getting him alone, he might be more willing to cough up a little more information—off the clock.

Paladin knelt and began to clean out a flat space on the dusty ground. He used his index finger to draw a schematic representation of the base that B.R.A.I.N. had sent him during their run-over. It was all he could do to show Thief what he was visualizing. Thief squatted as well.

"Okay. So here we have the main entrance to the base. And over here is the airfield, along with the garage. We are exactly here," Paladin said, pressing his index finger into the ground between the main entrance and the garage. "The barracks are over here." He made a small X just northwest of their position, about halfway beyond the front gate and the back perimeter. "There are cameras all along the fence, scattered some six to eight feet apart with guards patrolling the inside of the fence in groups of two to three. There's no real schedule at play."

"The randomness is intentional to throw off any planning."

Paladin nodded. "It'll be a little more difficult than I thought to slip in undetected."

"What if you boys had uniforms and a key-pass," Blurr said from behind.

Paladin stood in shock. "Karla?"

"I thought I felt a surge of speed coming over me," Thief said.

Blurr shifted her weight to one side and placed her hands on her hips, something Paladin had been quite attracted to lately as it did an excellent job of accentuating her womanly curves. She looked exceptionally stunning tonight in her newly-commissioned gear as well, cleaned pressed and shiny. Her body glimmered against the night's full moon. Paladin was sure Thief had taken notice too and a pang of jealousy pulsed through his heart, making a part of him want to wrap her waist in her cape.

"Figured," Blurr said. She pointed to a bag lying next to her feet. Paladin only assumed what the contents would be.

"How did you know—" Paladin started.

Blurr raised her hand and eyed her fingertips as if she could see them through her gold, forearm-length gloves. "That you two were planning this botched scheme? Chalk it up to accelerated hearing. Supersonic at that. Everything's been on ten lately, hearing included. Don't know why, but I'm not complaining. I can hear a flea fart. Besides, as usual, you two need my help. Again."

"So you were eavesdropping," Paladin said.

"Don't call it that," Blurr said. She paused and touched her forehead, staggering for a moment before catching her balance.

Paladin stepped forward and grabbed her by the arm. "The dizziness. It's back again?"

Blurr pulled away. "I'm fine," she said defensively. "And it's not eavesdropping. Consider it collecting Intel." Blurr whizzed in close to Paladin and moved his helmet to the side, exposing his face and planting a soft kiss on his lips all on one motion. After a few seconds, she pulled back.

Paladin noticed that Thief was staring off into space. "What was that for?" he whispered to Blurr.

"A token of appreciation. I heard when you threw that punch at Thief. You tried to fight for my dignity. It was crazy and foolish, yes.

But it's the kind of man I need in my life." She looked over at Thief. "One who is willing to sacrifice for me."

Thief looked over at them both. "Couldn't agree more, love. Now that you two lovebirds are done, can we get back to planning for this meeting?"

"Right," Paladin said, securing his helmet back in place.

Blurr walked over to the sketch on the floor and bumped Thief off-center as she did. She looked back at him. "And for the *record*, what we had was just a game. Nothing more."

Thief straightened and shot a look between Paladin and Blurr. He nodded respectfully. "Right, love."

Chapter 7
fissure

After completely ignoring the plan laid out by Blurr—which entailed the two of them donning the uniforms, entering the front gate and then heading straight for the officer's quarters in the barracks—Thief thought it safe to improvise and take the scenic route, leading Paladin by the Special R&D section of the base in the process. Wearing the infantry uniforms and donning a pair of caps made for a perfect disguise, all but entirely covering up their costumes. Paladin carried his helmet and gloves in his backpack while Thief had stuffed his Cowell in his pocket.

"This is just plain stupid," Paladin whispered, trailing Thief as they entered the R&D building. Thief hurried Paladin inside and shut the door behind them. The hallway was pristine, emanating an ominous clean sparkle that was half inviting and half eerie. In Paladin's mind, this degree of perfection was reserved for futuristic world-ending mad scientists and alien invaders.

"Come on, stop your complaining for once. We'll only get one shot at seeing what Uncle Sam is cooking up here, so we might as well use it to our advantage."

"Maybe it's best we do it some other time. We're here to visit with the Colonel, remember?"

Thief pointed a finger at him. "I do remember. But I also know that the good ole United States of America doesn't like to lend itself to the best honest practices. People find things out by doing their own research."

"Snooping counts as research all of a sudden, huh?"

"I thought you wanted answers."

"If you two are going to keep on with this the Odd Couple routine, I'm coming in there after you," Blurr's voice boomed over their inner earpiece communications systems.

"Yes, ma'am. We're moving out," Thief joked. Thief walked past Paladin in a hunched-over posture, hugging the nearby wall with his shoulder. Paladin followed suit. At the end of the hallway was a large, heavy-looking iron door with a green light affixed above it and a keypad in the place that the handle should be. "This must be the place."

"What must be the place?" Paladin asked.

"Again, another dossier I unearthed—"

"Stole."

"Whatever, while I was doing my research, spoke of such a place. At least in its description."

"Well, shouldn't there be some 'Authorized Personnel Only' sigh hanging outside of it?"

"One of my contacts said that most of the R&D bases keep things real discrete. You watch way too much TV, bucko."

"Just try the keypad, will you?"

Thief slipped the key pass through the slot along the side of the keypad and waited as series of numbers flashed along the small screen. Paladin prayed that they wouldn't have to enter any numbers. When the numbers stopped scrolling, the door jarred open, allowing a cool stream of air to pass outside.

"Bingo," Thief said, sounding equally as relieved as Paladin.

The two slipped inside with Paladin taking the lead, having donned his helmet and gloves while initiating his strength variant to protect them from impending danger. The room was dimly lit with twenty-foot ceilings dwarfing them on all four sides. The walls were of a shiny, silver luster that Paladin could only make out through his enhanced optics systems inside his helmet. He touched the wall with his fingertips. "Cool, smooth and—" He paused as his fingers sunk into the metal surface. "Malleable?"

Thief touched it too. "More like gooey," he said as his fingers disappeared in the substance up to his knuckles. He pulled his hand free as his eyes swept the rest of the room. They landed on a large glass tank some twenty feet away. "Check that out," he said with a nod.

Paladin followed his eyes and watched as Thief ran over to investigate. "Wait," Paladin cautioned. The tank was filled with a black mist that swirled around at a slow, steady speed. Neither one of them could make out anything or anyone within the dark cloud. Thief seemed oddly engaged, almost to the point of panic by the sight of it. "You okay?" Paladin asked.

"No. There's something in the tank."

"Yeah, I got that. Black smoke."

"No. It's something else. Dark Matter."

"Dark Matter? How the hell can the U.S. military contain something we barely know anything about?"

"Because it's the military. Just because they tell us *we* know nothing, doesn't mean that *they* know nothing."

"True. So what does this mean?"

"Don't know. Can you get a couple of shots of this?"

"I'm scanning and uploading the images to B.R.A.I.N. as we speak. Can we get out here and visit the Colonel before someone detects us?"

"Yeah…sure," Thief said, still eyeing the tank intently.

"Guys, I've got a pair of guards coming your way down that hallway. Make a move," Lydia said.

"Oh, now you're watching too?" Paladin asked.

"The minute you started your shenanigans, B.R.A.I.N. alerted me, so I just looked on," Lydia said.

"What are you, Big Brother?" Paladin said.

"Big Cousin. Get moving," Lydia said.

"Exit strategy?" Paladin asked.

"Back door, twenty feet, key pass access, quickly," Lydia said.

Thief grabbed Paladin by the waist and sped to the door, slipping the key pass through the slot at light speed. The door unlocked and the two of them were outside before the guards could gain entry. Paladin snatched Thief by the arm and jumped to the roof of the building, landing with a thud. He looked off in the direction of the barracks. "Now can we go?"

"Following your lead," Thief said.

The two men raced across the rooftop and bounded two more on their way to the barracks. Safely atop that building too, Paladin relayed the probable position of Colonel Matheson to Thief as quickly as Lydia uploaded the information to him. Thief searched the sides of the four-story building as quickly as possible, looking for a safe entry point. "Third floor, huh" he murmured. "Okay, this should do nicely." He leaned off the backside of the building, glaring at an open window. "If you can pick up enough speed, we can slip in through that room and make our move."

"If we run into trouble—"

"Don't worry, I'll take them down quietly," Paladin said with a smile.

"What about gorgeous back there? What's all that dizzy stuff about?" Thief asked.

"Nothing," Paladin said. Deep inside, his level of concern for Karla was beginning to swell, but he didn't want Thief to know. He was her man now. Taking care of her was his job, and that's the way he wanted it to stay. "Can you focus here for a moment? We have a job to do."

"To the job," Thief said, throwing a salute Paladin's way.

Jumping from the ledge, the two speedsters slipped into the window and made their way inside the room. They were met by two infantry troopers who were unarmed, but wearing shoulder comms that made them just as dangerous. "Who are you two?" one of them asked.

Thief zipped behind both of them and gave a quick slap to the back of their cervical spines, dropping them like flies. They dragged them into the bathroom and approached the door. "The helmet, take it off," Thief said.

Paladin removed his helmet, and Thief opened the door to the hallway. "Left," Paladin said.

They walked the hallway as naturally as two intruders could, doing their best to act normal. Paladin, however, was no actor, nursing a stream of sweat that was slowly drizzling down his back. But Thief, on the other hand, seemed to be right at home snooping around like this. Chalk it up to either his detective ways or his shady past, Paladin wasn't sure. But he envied him a little at this juncture. Losing ahold of the situation and getting caught could be catastrophic at this point, not just for the current team, but the possible future of the F.R.I.E.N.D.S. Initiative. As soldiers walked by, making eye contact, Paladin's nerves were beginning to get the best of him. "Another right," he barked.

A couple of soldiers paused and looked at them.

Thief caught on and flashed a smile, apparently noticing the men's restroom off in the corner. "I know where the john is, idiot. Keep your junk in your pants. I got first dibs. I've been holding it all night on that shift."

The soldiers shared a smile with him and continued walking. As the soldiers exited the hallway and rounded the corner, Thief and Paladin pressed on, clearing two more turns before coming to the Officer's Quarters. They were met by a door and a guard sitting at a desk, diligently writing on a pad. Thief approached. "Hi, Lak-it-sym?" he asked, reading the name on his badge slowly.

"Lakitsym. What can I do for you?" the guard barked.

"Colonel Matheson in?" Thief asked.

The soldier looked up, wearing a rather inquisitive look on his face. "Who's asking?"

"HQ is. They sent me and corporal Stetson here to escort him in. They're having an emergency meeting," Thief said.

The soldier's eyes danced between the two of them. "Colonel Matheson hasn't been in all day. I think he retired for the night." He stood. "I'm going to need to see some clearance paperwork. Nobody enters through this door—"

Before the soldier could say another word, Thief grabbed him by the collar, jerked him forward, and clapped him over the back of the neck, knocking him out cold. If Paladin wasn't paying close attention, he'd have missed the entire show, seeing how quickly Thief had moved.

"You're getting good at that," Paladin said.

Thief dragged the soldier to the corner and dusted off his hands. "Yeah. Learned a thing or two overseas."

"You gotta show me sometime."

"No, I don't."

Paladin shook his head. "You're so petty sometimes."

"He won't stay out long. Let's get inside."

Thief and Paladin pushed through the door and entered. The space was a good size, some twenty feet long, complete with a full kitchen, sitting room and two doors on the opposite side. Various portraits of Colonel Matheson filled the walls. Women, men, fellow soldiers, and children painted their view. "This your guy?" Thief asked.

"Yeah, that's him," Paladin said. "But where is he?"

"Door number one or two?"

"After you," Paladin said.

Thief ran to the door on the right and opened it. A man fell to the floor face first. The sound of his skull smacking the floor made a sickening sound. Thief knelt beside him, looking up at Paladin with a look of concern.

"Matheson," Paladin said faintly.

Thief felt his neck for a pulse. "Was…Matheson." He examined a red abrasion encircling Matheson's neck. "Strangulation."

"What? But how? Who?"

"Body's cold. Must have been a couple of days." Thief's eyes widened. "Get that guard, now!"

Paladin ran to the door and quickly opened it, but the soldier was nowhere to be found. The sound of an alarm blared overhead. Paladin slipped back inside and shut the door, using his speed to twist the handle until it fused into one solid piece. He leaned his head to the door. "Footsteps. We got trouble."

"Dead Colonel, absconding soldier. You bet we do."

The sound of kicks against the door caught both of their attention. "Put some fire on that door, soldier!" a loud voice screamed.

Paladin slapped on his helmet, and Thief donned his Cowll. Bullets pelted the door until it finally gave way, falling into the room. Soldier charged in and trained their guns on Paladin and Thief. Before they could shoot, Thief had sprung into action, relieving them of their handguns. Paladin followed close behind, making quick work of their holstered weapons as well. As more soldiers entered, Paladin and Thief continued their unarming dance until a strong whirlwind filled the room, lifting everyone and pinning them against the walls. The miniature tornado continued to churn, snatching portraits, furniture and anything else not pinned down in its wake.

When the cyclone finally stopped, everyone fell to the floor and only Blurr remained standing in the center. The soldiers—dazed from the maneuver—gazed at her in awe. Blurr adjusted her goggles and raked her fingers through her hair. "Down, boys. We're not here to cause trouble."

An officer stood. "Ma'am, if you mean us no harm, then why is our colonel dead," he said, pointing at Matheson's cold body.

"Where's the guard?" Paladin asked, addressing the officer.

"What guard? Nobody guards Colonel Matheson's quarters," the officer replied.

"The guard. Why didn't I see it," Thief said in disgust.

"See what?" Paladin asked.

"His name. It wasn't Lakitsym. It's Mystikal spelled backward. That fool was playing us," Thief said.

Paladin stepped forward, handing the officer back his handgun.

"Officer Burks, there's been a terrible mistake, and I feel this base has been compromised. A very dangerous Super-Normal by the name of Mystikal is on the loose. I'm afraid he's been posing as Colonel Matheson. He came by my...*base* the other day. With two or three other soldiers."

"That's odd. Colonel Matheson hasn't been off base in days," Officer Burks said.

"Apparently," Thief said.

"So, Mystikal was Matheson. That means that the other soldiers with him were created by Mirage," Blurr said.

"Girl's good," Thief said. "My detective skills are rubbing off on you."

"That's all that'll be rubbing off on me ever again," Blurr said.

"Touché, baby," Thief said.

"Can you take us to the next highest-ranking officer on base, Officer Burks?" Paladin asked.

"Sure, that'll be Admiral Hankerson. Come this way," Officer Burks said.

***

Moments later, Paladin, Blurr, and Thief found themselves standing in front of a tribunal of high ranking officials—Admiral Hankerson in the middle with two other gentlemen seated to his right and left—answering questions leading from the night of Colonel Matheson's visit up until his untimely death.

"You mean to tell me that a Super-Normal is running around this facility stealing Intel?" a dark-skinned man sitting on the right asked.

"Absolutely. Sad thing is, it could be on you, Lieutenant Dixon," Paladin said.

"Or you," Lieutenant Dixon retorted.

"This is true. Only we know who *we* are. So I vouch for these two. The real McCoys, I promise," Blurr said.

"How can you be so sure?" Admiral Hankerson asked.

"They got caught," Blurr said with a snide smile. "True *thieves* never get caught. If I hadn't come in when I did, they'd probably be cannon fodder. Besides, if you check your camera feeds, you see exactly when they entered the Officer's Quarters and entered Colonel Matheson's room."

"I thought Lydia killed the feeds," Paladin said.

"She rerouted the feeds back to *base*. Figured she'd keep them just in case we needed any proof against wrongdoing. When you guys are involved, we always need an alibi," Blurr said.

"Which leads us back to you all, Admiral," Thief said.

"We've been in a meeting all night. No one in or out. Your arrival here today is a funny coincidence. We are in need of your services. In our meeting, we were discussing what you've already been briefed on by whoever Colonel Matheson really was. The F.R.I.E.N.D.S. Initiative," Admiral Hankerson said. He pointed a remote at the wall behind Thief. "Along with this." The wall opened and a screen dropped down. The screen flickered and then filled with the still image of an asteroid hurling through space. Admiral Hankerson clicked a button on the remote again and the image zoomed in closer. "This is a recording of a live feed from one hour ago."

The asteroid was dazzling, glimmering, and sparkling as if it were covered in pure gold and diamonds. "Wow. Now that's a girl's best friend," Blurr said, staring.

"It's just a huge rock. Not of much value," Thief said.

"Don't feel threatened, guys. You just can't measure up to a large sparkly," Blurr joked.

"I'm afraid Blurr is right. This is no ordinary rock," Admiral Hankerson said. "But it is a huge threat to planet Earth."

"Threat, Admiral," Paladin asked.

"Three weeks ago, scientists began to track a large object entering our solar system just outside of Pluto. It's cleared thousands of miles at a record pace. This asteroid has been on a clear collision course with our planet ever since and has not veered. Not even for a minute," Admiral Hankerson said.

"How big is it?" Thief asked.

"That's where things get interesting," the man to the left of Admiral Hankerson said. "I'm Captain Terringer. The asteroid is currently outside of Jupiter, but a convoy and I intercepted it outside of the rings of Saturn."

"Intercepted it? How so?" Blurr asked.

"NASA built a supersonic deep space vessel named the U.S.S.

Overdrive, capable of warp travel in short bursts," Captain Terringer said. "It was a prototype of one they are working to perfect, and we decided to give it a trial run. It was a big sacrifice, but I felt it was worth it. And it paid off. My crew and I met the asteroid and fired three concussive blasts of high-grade Gamma Lasers at it, decimating about ninety percent of it. The warp cores on the ship proved to only be good enough to get us back home. We wanted to track the asteroid but simply ran out of juice. This piece you see here is the last of the asteroid, approximately the size of a Volkswagen."

"Doesn't sound like much of a threat to the planet, even if it hits the planet at tremendous speeds," Thief said.

"It's not the size of the asteroid we're concerned about. It's the content," Lieutenant Dixon added.

"This asteroid is named Q-18 Exitium," Admiral Hankerson said. "Exitium is Latin for destruction. It is very, very, very valuable. It's made of nothing but precious metals; rubies, diamonds, emeralds, gold, platinum, etc. Even at its current size and density, it's valued at one quintillion."

"Quin-what?" Paladin asked.

"Put it this way. Start with a one and add eighteen zeroes," Admiral Hankerson said.

"Whoa," Blurr said.

"Unbelievable! That word really exists?" Paladin asked.

Admiral Hankerson nodded. "As real as the air in this room."

"The threat...where do we come in?" Thief asked.

"A stone of this value creates a large problem in our current global state. Countries are at war. There is civil unrest, famine, and poverty everywhere. Just one ounce of this rock can immediately rejuvenate the economy of several countries," Lieutenant Dixon said.

"That'd be a good thing, right? I mean, people all over the world can finally receive supplies they need to eat. To live. Medications can be delivered. Lives can be saved," Paladin said.

"If only the world worked like that," Lieutenant Dixon said. "The word has already gotten out about Q-18. We received Intel that hundreds of countries are already amassing armies and black market weapons to stage a massive assault on the impact site of Q-18. Only military sects of these countries seem to know of it, so we don't—as of yet—have any concerns for civilian involvement. Still, we're talking about a war of epic proportions. World War Three scale. This will potentially cause a fissure in already-melting thin ice of peace we're all skating on. People aren't trying to help the world. Military leaders are vying to take it down. With that much money in the hands of a dictator, there's no limit to the army he could build. And with the economy booming, he could run the planet and no one could contain him."

"And so I ask again, Lieutenant, where do *we* come in?" Thief spat in a low tone.

"We, the United States of America, need you to go to the impact site, hold off anyone who attempts to capture the asteroid, and remove it from the planet. For good," Admiral Hankerson said.

"For good?" Blurr asked.

"I will be there, as well. Once you are able to secure the asteroid, we need to take it aboard the Overdrive and then I will take it back into space and hit it with one more blast of the Gamma Lasers," Captain Terringer said. "Traveling at that speed and size, it would take about four to five days to cool enough for anyone to touch it. But NASA developed a cooling foam that will speed up the process. We'll need about three minutes."

"Three minutes. You won't have three seconds once the word gets out. We'll have everyone and their mama trying to take a swipe at it," Thief said with a smirk.

Suddenly, his face flattened and his demeanor shifted to a more serious tone as a thought pierced his mind.

He looked over at Paladin, who immediately picked up on it and slowly uttered, "Everyone…including Super-Normals."

Chapter 8
COUNTDOWN

"So exactly how much time are we looking at here, Admiral?" Paladin asked.

"If Q-18 continues its present course, we'll be looking at an impact of about two days from now. We'll provide all the transportation and resources you need to be successful," Admiral Hankerson said.

"We've already mobilized the U.S.S. Overdrive. It should be at the impact site by tomorrow," Captain Terringer said.

"And where exactly is that?" Thief asked.

Admiral Hankerson chuckled. "You're going to love this. The South Pole."

"Santa," Thief chirped.

"That's the North Pole, goofball," Paladin said.

"Oh. Pardon me. I didn't celebrate Christmas," Thief said.

"A fight for a blinging ice on *top* of ice. Come on, Admiral. You're making that up," Blurr said.

"I really wish we were, darling. But this is not a joke," Admiral Hankerson said.

"Okay, but it's the South Pole, Admiral. No one has a solitary stake in it, right?" Paladin asked.

"Precisely right, Paladin," Admiral Hankerson said. "As of this moment, both the North and South Poles are considered free due to their nutrient-rich land. On record, only in a case of depleted resources

102

are any countries allowed to extract from them. Off record, the USA, UK, Russia, Australia, Argentina, Chile, France, Norway, and New Zealand all have strong claims to it, from a scientific standpoint."

"So we could be looking at eight counties getting involved?" Blurr asked.

"That seems to complicate things a bit, huh," Thief said.

"Not so much. Intelligence counts less. If we're lucky. It's a neutral territory, but we've already had assets on the ground, so we'll be in strong force. It's actually better that it's neutral because, if it wasn't, we'd be looking at World War III because no one would be respecting borders," Admiral Hankerson said. His eyes hovered over all three of the Super-Normals. "The United States needs your help. All of you."

Paladin stared at Blurr. She wore a flat guise that he couldn't get a read on. It was times like these that he was fortunate to don a helmet so that he could stay hidden. Surely, the epitome of fear was written all over his face, but he couldn't let her see him sweat. Not now. Not while Thief was present. From what he'd already seen and experienced, Thief was a gambler and a pretty damn good bluffer at that. He couldn't look weak, not now. The leader of their trio of Super-Normals hadn't been officially decided yet, and he had no intention of handing the title over to Thief by default. More importantly, he wouldn't dare look anything less than brave in Karla's eyes.

How was she holding up with all this big news? *Come on, Karla, give me a sign or something*, he thought.

"What's in it for us?" Thief asked aloud.

"Saving the world. Saving yourselves in the process. What else would you need?" Admiral Hankerson asked.

Thief folded his arms. "Seems to me like this would be a good time to play Let's Make a Deal or something like that."

He had balls, Paladin had to give him that. And what was he working at anyway? Certainly, the government would provide New Chicago with additional funding. But Thief wasn't known to be altruistic by any means. So there had to be something more. Something more self-centered.

"What, a hero's parade," Paladin guessed, mocking Thief.

"No," Thief barked rather abruptly. "I want anonymity for my ex-wife and my kids. As a matter of fact, all of her family too. They didn't ask to be dragged into this freak show of a life I'm living now, and I know how the mentally disturbed power-mongers of the world operate. They'll latch on to our families and do things—nasty things—as payback for stripping them of an opportunity for endless wealth. Payback's a bitch."

Blurr stood motionless as if she had momentarily stopped breathing. Paladin held his breath too, waiting a moment or two to see if she would respond. But what she didn't say in her words, she screamed in her face. His words had affected her, crushing some part of her soul that she had reserved for hating him. At that moment, she saw what Paladin had admittedly thought inconceivable, too. Thief actually…cared?

"Sounds like a plan to me," Admiral Hankerson said.

Captain Terringer clapped his hands. "It's settled. We'll mobilize immediately."

"Not so fast," Thief said. "One more thing, Admiral."

The Admiral's face waxed cold. "Yes, Thief?"

"Q-18. When we send it into space, I want it destroyed. Totally. Not an ounce of that rock makes it back to Earth. Are we clear?"

Admiral Hankerson flashed a flat smile. "Crystal...son."

Lieutenant Dixon walked over to Thief, holding out a white card with black writing on it. "I take it you're in charge?"

Paladin butt in. "Uh, that's not decided yet."

"Yes, it has been," Blurr said, zipping by and taking the card from his hand. "I'm the leader. These two think with the wrong heads most times."

"Don't we all," Lieutenant Dixon said jokingly. "That's the address for the pickup spot. We'll see you all tomorrow at 2300 hours. Don't be late."

"Dismissed," Admiral Hankerson said. "You're welcome to stay the night. The base is secure, we assure you that."

"Nah," Paladin said. "With Mystikal at large, we can't be one hundred percent sure of that. Besides, we have some last-minute preparations to make at base. You know, leadership stuff."

"In that case, we'll have our men escort you off the base," Admiral Hankerson said.

"Not a problem," Paladin said.

"And team," Admiral Hankerson said. "What Matheson or Mystikal told you about the F.R.I.E.N.D.S. Initiative was no lie. It's coming."

***

Thief, Sebastian, and Karla left the military base and headed back to Sebastian's penthouse. Inside, they all sat around the living room table trying to make perfect sense of the night's activity. Bringing Lydia up to speed was nothing short of a nightmare. After finding Colonel Matheson's body, Paladin had cut all communications to her to think straight. Always having a second voice in your head was a bit of a nightmare at times.

"Wow. So we still don't know where Mirage and Mystikal are," Lydia said. "Like, they could be any one of us."

Sebastian thought it was cute to play along. "Yeah, and maybe even this entire ordeal is some crazy concocted illusion whipped up by Mirage to make us follow through with some hidden agenda he has."

"Right," Lydia replied. When she noticed the others flashing one another smirks, she finally caught on to Sebastian's sarcasm. She swatted at Sebastian from across the couch. "Not funny, punk."

"Honestly, think about it for a minute. When fake Matheson was here, notice how he didn't shake anyone's hand. And those military goons never touched anything. At first, I just thought they were germophobes, but now it all makes sense. If they were holograms drummed up by Mirage, they couldn't interact with anything," Karla said.

"And that one creep made a move on you. Remember how Matheson—I mean Mystikal—yelled at him? That was probably Mirage himself," Lydia said.

"But why come here? For recon?" Sebastian asked.

"Maybe," Thief said.

"They did ask where you were," Sebastian said.

"Most likely trying to get a head-count," Karla said.

"If Mystikal and Mirage were that deep in the military, there's no telling who else knows now," Paladin said. "This is pretty bad."

"Oh, it gets worse," Thief said.

"Thanks, sunshine," Sebastian said.

"Across seas—" Thief started.

"You came across a dossier, we know," Paladin said, cutting him off. But no one laughed. "Sorry."

Thief shook his head. "I came across some *Intel* that The Majesties had found Albert Bernstein. And we all know that's horse manure because Bernstein aka Caine, Slash, Mr. Magnificent is dead."

"Mystikal again, Alice?" Lydia asked.

Thief wagged a firm finger at her. "Don't...ever say that name again," his voice boomed.

"Right. I...I just wanted to try it out. I love the name, actually. It won't happen again," Lydia said nervously.

"What did The Majesties say Bernstein was doing?" Paladin asked.

"Not a lot of information on that, per se," Thief started. "When I saw it, I knew it had to be a smokescreen, so I followed a few leads in hopes to find more on Bernstein's super-soldier research. I came up empty on that, but that's when I came across the dossier on Titan and the artifact."

"See, I knew you'd say the dossier line," Sebastian said.

Lydia hit Sebastian again. "Stop playing, Sebas. Thief is serious now and, well, I'm kinda scared of him. Whoops, did I say that out loud?"

"Yeah, no inner earpiece communication system on, cousin," Sebastian said.

"Big moves in the Middle East, activity up in space, and diamonds raining from the sky in a matter of two days. Anybody else up for placing bets on cows jumping over the moon or hell freezing over," Karla joked.

"So, are we really gonna do this, team?" Lydia asked.

The question fell on a room of dead silence. Sebastian couldn't hide behind his helmet anymore, nor Karla her nonchalant attitude, nor Thief his toughness. How they felt was all out in the open for every one of them to see.

"This is as good a time as any to back out," Sebastian said.

"No time for fake ones," Karla said. "I'm in."

Sebastian looked at Thief. Fittingly, the spotlight was on him; just as he had made an astounding introduction to the people of New Chicago as a murderer that started the train of events sparking their teaming up, all success of the next phase of their partnership hinged on his decision. If they had any shot of hope in protecting Q-18 and turning back any opposition with plans to obtain its extravagant wealth, Thief would have to be on board.

"I'm in, too. What else do I have to live for," Thief said finally, raising a glass of wine.

"What about our position? Should we stay here or bolt?" Karla asked.

"Thief asked why we hadn't moved into The Beacon. With this location compromised, seems like a good a time as any to cut bait and head on over," Sebastian suggested.

"Probably so. But we still don't know what the state of that place is now. For all we know, Mirage could be over there now hiding behind some fake wall. We'd walk right into a trap," Thief said.

"It's not like we have much time anyway. We roll out in the morning," Lydia said.

"*We*, cousin," Sebastian asked, raising an eyebrow at Lydia.

Lydia placed her hands on her hips. "Oh, I know you don't expect me to stay *here*."

"Is it that bad?" B.R.A.I.N. asked.

Lydia looked up. "Oh, no, it's not like that B.R.A.I.N., I was just saying I don't feel safe anymore."

"Sounds like it's exactly like *that* to me," B.R.A.I.N. replied. "I took the liberty of scrubbing the place down with an infrared scan while you all were chatting. Place is clean as a whistle. No bugs or taps. If they had intentions of spying on us from the start, they must've had reservations."

"Or planned to come back later when they had a better plan," Karla said.

"Or when they thought I was back," Thief added.

Sebastian approached Lydia. "Cousin, I still don't like it. We don't know what to expect out there. This is an insane event and an even crazier idea for us to throw ourselves in feet first."

"Then why do it, Sebas?" Lydia asked.

Sebastian's eyes swept over the room, landing on Thief first, and then pausing on Karla. His heart skipped as she locked eyes with his. "Because, well, I don't think we really have a choice in the matter. The people of Earth are depending on us."

"Great. Then you know why I have to be there with you. You're the last bit of family I have. And staying here will drive me absolutely batty. I have to be there with you." She glanced over at Thief and Karla and flashed them both a smile. "With all of you. I'll patch B.R.A.I.N. through to my laptop and operate out of some army vehicle. I'm sure they'll give me what I need to be your eyes and ears." She took Sebastian by the wrists. "We're more than a family. We're a team."

How could Sebastian deny her? "Well, if B.R.A.I.N. promises to keep us all patched in, then I guess you can go. It's not like you're going to listen to me anyway."

"You know me so well," Lydia said.

"Countdown is on. Let's make plans to lay it down, *team*. We need to get prepped to roll out bright and early," Thief said.

The team began to disperse and Lydia motioned Thief over to

where she was. "I've got a room ready for you Al—I mean, Thief."

Thief didn't reply, but headed toward her and wagged his finger silently. Sebastian and Karla were alone.

"Can I talk to you for a moment? In private?" Karla asked.

"Sure," Sebastian said, ushering her upstairs to his bedroom.

When they climbed the stairs, Sebastian followed Karla over to a window and stood behind her. She gazed out over the city in a daze. Sebastian waited a few seconds, and when the silence between them got too strong, he closed the distance and rested his hands firmly on her shoulders. "What is it?" he asked in a hushed tone.

"I…I don't know what to think of all this," Karla said.

"If it helps any, I don't either. A few months ago, I was only thinking about solving a murder mystery and saving the city. Never did I imagine it'd grow to saving the planet."

Karla turned to him. Her eyes were glossy. "It's not that."

"Not that? What is it, then?"

"I've been having these visions when I'm awake and dreams when I'm sleeping. I see things. Fluctuations in time. People I knew from before and some other folks that I don't recognize, but I feel as if I know them. Like I've seen them before."

"Anyone I know?"

"I can only remember flashes. I see you, Lydia, and Thief. My old family. And…others. Aliens."

Sebastian recalled the dream he had earlier of Karla being captured and taken away, all while he fell back to Earth in a failed attempt to save her. "What aliens?"

"I don't see faces, just their technology. Beautiful, massive ships that glide through the skies. They move just as fast as us, if not faster."

"Do they hurt you?"

"No. Actually, I feel like I know them. You know that feeling you get in your stomach when you're around family having a good time?"

"Can't say I've ever experienced that. Maybe with you, but that's all."

"Sorry. Well, it's kinda like that. I can't explain it, but I just don't think they were there to harm me. It's more like they came to save me."

"Those feelings could be misinterpreted, Karla. All this military talk of beings from another planet with an agenda. Doesn't sound like family to me."

Karla hung her head. "I know."

"Was there anything else about these dreams that you can recall?"

"I sensed a heavy amount of pain. Not physical pain but of loss. Like I'm losing something. That the more powerful I become, the more I lose touch with those who care about me."

"Like me?"

Karla nodded. "Yes."

Sebastian took her by the shoulders. "That's not gonna happen. I'm never leaving you, Karla. Got that?"

"I know you won't. I still can't explain why you're so in love with me, but I'm grateful."

"Love doesn't require an explanation. Just know that I do. When we go out to the impact site, promise me one thing?"

"Yes, my love?"

"That when the fighting starts—and there will be lots of it—you'll concentrate on that, not me. I can't afford for you to divide your attention. I'll be watching your back."

"I can't promise you such a thing."

"Karla, I know people think that Thief is the most powerful Super-Normal next to Mr. Magnificent, but I beg to differ. I think the true power lies inside of you. Your speed power can be anything. Power. Strength. Agility. All those things are factors that made Mr. Magnificent what he was. You have all of those qualities, and you're only getting stronger. I can see it in you."

"Then why do I feel so weak? I've been having these dizzy spells lately. And they're getting more and more infrequent. More like daily."

"You didn't tell me that."

"How could I? I know you'd worry."

"It's my job to worry. You can't shut me out. Have you told Lydia about it?"

"Yeah. She believes what you do. That my powers are growing, and that the portal through the dimensions of space and time are beginning to merge. I no longer just see one thing; I can see both. And not just see them but experience them."

"That's exciting."

"Only to those on the sidelines. When I go through those dizzy spells, I see everything—past, present, and future merging. And my brain can't keep pace. That's why I feel like I'm about to fall. The only thing that keeps me sane is the speed. My body craves it now, more than being still or at rest."

"That's why you're having so much trouble sleeping, isn't it?"

"I'm afraid so." Karla sat on the edge of the bed.

Sebastian followed. He held her hand. "Whatever this is, we will get through it. I'm here with you. And you've got a team around you. When this is over, maybe we can reach out to The Majesties to see what their take on it is. Maybe Slaycick has gone through it and can possibly shine some light on it."

Tears began to flow from Karla's eyes. "Okay."

Sebastian wiped them from the corners and lifted her chin as he pressed his lips to hers. They held it for a few seconds, until being interrupted by B.R.A.I.N.

"Sebas, I've got a little surprise for you. Come into the laboratory."

'Seriously, B.R.A.I.N.? Can't it wait? I'm a little busy," Sebastian said.

"Not really," B.R.A.I.N. said.

Karla touched the side of Sebastian's face. "Let's see what he's rambling about."

Sebastian and Karla stood and walked over to the laboratory. A glass casing slowly lowered from the ceiling and landed on the tile floor. The lights dimmed theatrically and a green 3D image of what appeared to be the S3.1 appeared before them. "Behold, the S4,"

B.R.A.I.N. said.

"S4?" Sebastian asked.

"Strength, stealth, speed, and *mind*. All combined for seamless transitioning between variants," B.R.A.I.N. said.

The glass case opened with a hiss and steam seeped from the edges as the door rose, revealing a brand new version of the suit, similar in design with slight changes in the architecture. If Sebastian hadn't been so well acquainted with the previous ones, he'd barely notice the difference.

Sebastian stepped forward and touched it. "Man, it sure is pretty, sir," he said in a country twang.

A robotic arm lowered from the ceiling and a long needle extended from its pincers. "Drop your chin, Sebastian," B.R.A.I.N. said.

"What's that?" Sebastian asked, staring at the needle.

"It's a microscopic nanobot. It will penetrate your spine and make its way into your midbrain," B.R.A.I.N. said.

Sebastian waved his hands. "Uh, you lost me at penetrate," Sebastian said.

"It will make the necessary connection between the higher cognitive layers of your brain and the suit," B.R.A.I.N. said. "You'll be able to operate it at a subconscious level. When you're afraid, the stealth or speed variant will activate. When you're angry, you may call on strength. It's all situational."

"That's pretty cool," Karla said.

Sebastian looked over at her. "You want to try it out?"

Karla walked over to Sebastian and caressed the sides of his face. "Stand still. I'm here with you."

Sebastian closed his eyes and slowly lowered his head as she gently guided him. The robotic arm closed in, and the pincers aimed directly at the base of Sebastian's skull. The needle pierced his skin, making him twitch, but Karla's grip tightened, giving him just the right amount of reassurance he needed. He felt a quick tap on his neck and the robotic arm pulled away.

Sebastian opened his eyes and touched the back of his head. The smell of smoke stung his nose. "Did you cook me?"

"No, just seared you a little. It was necessary to close the wound. The nanobot is making its way along as we speak. I hope you don't *mind*," B.R.A.I.N. said.

"That's funny. B.R.A.I.N., real funny," Sebastian said.

Karla giggled. "Do you feel it?"

"Not an ounce," Sebastian said.

"Sync complete," B.R.A.I.N. announced. "Go ahead, give the S4 a whirl."

"What do you mean?" Sebastian asked.

"Just, *think* about it," B.R.A.I.N. said.

"About what?" Sebastian asked.

"About what you want it to do," B.R.A.I.N. answered.

Sebastian scratched his forehead. "Uh, okay."

In a flash, the S4 came alive, leaped from the glass casing, and wrapped around Sebastian, and the helmet fell to the floor. Before long, it had folded itself around his entire torso, arms, and legs. Sebastian held his hands before his face and eyed his forearms and thighs. "Not the most comfortable fit."

"That's because you have clothes on, doll," Karla said. "When you strip down to your undies, it'll be a different story."

Sebastian picked up the helmet and slid it over his head. A new HUD greeted him, offering normal, thermal, X-ray, or infrared vision options. Intuitively, all Sebastian had to do was think about which variant he wanted to use, and the suit willfully obliged. "Whoa! That was cool." He pointed at Karla. "I can see your panties."

"That's a lie. I'm not wearing any."

"T.M.I.," B.R.A.I.N. said. "You are fully functional. Test thirty-eight now complete. Systems running at approximately ninety-eight percent."

"Let's not play any games this time. I think I'll need those last two," Sebastian said.

"Don't worry. Come 2300 tomorrow, you'll have all of it. You'll be ready," B.R.A.I.N. said.

ACT III

"In life, it's easy to be successful if you live every circumstance as though it were a moment on the battlefield, very similar to the quarter positions of a clock. Keep your enemies at your twelve, comrades, friends and family at your three and nine, and your past at your six. If you fail to do so, you'll lose your support and possibly be betrayed, misled, and deluded into thinking you've escaped your failures, only to be led into the clutches of your adversary."

Notes from the last speech given by gold standard to the Boys and Girls Club of Chicago

Chapter 9
appointment

900 HOURS

The next morning, Sebastian slid from his bed and stood, aroused by the chatter of two female voices and one lowly male one coming from downstairs. A male voice? How had he forgotten about Thief's new addition into the group was mind-boggling. Yes, he knew they needed his special skillset and he was grateful for Alice's return, but his male ego counterpart hated his inclusion, knowing full well that Thief was no sidekick. Thief's pride meter ran at twenty out of ten at all times and demanded the attention be placed squarely on his shoulders. He wouldn't share it, not for basic on-looking Normals and especially not for Karla, the latter being the piece of the puzzle Sebastian cared most about.

The celebrity of being a Super-Normal, earning seven-figure endorsements, and signing autographs was a passing fancy that had already worn thin in Sebastian's mind. The only thing he truly cared about was Karla. Ever since hearing the news about the potential of global tyranny with the arrival of Q-18, twelve or so probable outcomes had showered his headspace, making him contemplate multiple exit strategies that included either escaping to an uninhabited island or even a planet in another galaxy. Heck, it wasn't like he didn't have the coins at his disposal. His stock in drones has skyrocketed tenfold with the rise in popularity of *The Nightwatch* over the past year alone, quadrupling his already fat bank stash.

As much as he would have wanted to share this amazing news with Karla, something inside of him held back, fearful that either the news would make her stay just for the come-up or push her away due to her anxiety of feeling as though she wasn't good enough to be with someone like him. Not sure of how she'd react, he kept it to himself and awaited the right time to unveil the news that her man was currently the second richest soul on the planet.

Sebastian galloped down the stairs and joined the group as they crowded around the couch, preoccupied with whatever was playing on the news.

"Good day, Hero City, and welcome to another show. I'm Darla Cohanger," the female anchor said. She turned from the camera toward her cohost.

"And I'm Ryan Darlington," the male anchor said, gazing at the camera. "We come to you live with this amazing breaking news. Several people called in to report this earlier and we now have live footage to confirm the truth. It appears that there is indeed a new villain in town."

"The self-proclaimed 'Widget Man' made his appearance early this morning. Witnesses say he threw several occupied vehicles from the Du Sable Bridge," Darla said.

"The dark-gray suited villain, wearing what can only be described as a Hazmat helmet and respirator over his mouth, with large eye sockets that resemble those of a bee, killed a reported eight people thus far and is now standing atop the old statue of Mr. Magnificent in Grant Park," Ryan said. "We have live footage coming in now."

The camera flashed black and then opened again to the image of a female field reporter holding a microphone and shouting over the constant sound of wind whirling in the background. She attempted to clear her hair from her face. "Yes, Ryan. We are here at Grant Park where authorities say that Widget Man was sighted spearing multiple victims in the neck with tiny darts no larger than your index finger. There have been between twenty and thirty victims so far. Half of those people have been announced dead on site, and the other half are being transported to the hospital. As you can see behind me, the police are attempting to subdue the suspect with semi and automatic weapons to no avail. The bullets are merely bouncing off a small force field enveloping Widget Man. All efforts have failed at this point, and Widget Man is calling for the remaining heroes to join his side now before it is too late."

"Cheney, what appears to be the motive behind that?" Darla asked.

"It's unknown at this point, but we are all holding our breath waiting for the heroes to appear," Cheney said.

Just then, Widget Man turned his attention Cheney's way and pointed a hand in her direction. "Cheney, get outta there!" Ryan screamed.

Before she could move, a series of darts flew in her direction and pelted her from behind, tumbling over the cameraman as well. The news feed ended suddenly.

The picture returned to a shocked Darla and Ryan. As multiple staff came to their aid on live television, Karla turned off the TV. "Time to roll!"

Sebastian looked around. "Where's Thief?"

"He already left. Stole a shot of speed before he exited," Karla said. She darted up the stairs in a flash and zipped back down before Sebastian could take a breath, donning her complete costume.

The wind knocked over a glass of orange juice that Lydia was holding. "Hey!"

Blurr tossed the S4 to Sebastian. "Catch up," she said as she sped out a window that B.R.A.I.N. had opened.

Sebastian tossed the S4 in the air and began to run toward the window, raising his helmet to his head. The S4 floated behind, giving chase as if it had a mind of its own.

Lydia screamed in the background. "Sebastian, wait!"

By the time Sebastian hit the window, the S4 had already completely wrapped around his torso, pelvis and legs, with only his arms, hands, and neck showing. He jumped from the ledge, cycling his arms and legs as hard as he could. Seconds later, as his body began to descend to the city streets below, the S4 had completely woven itself around him.

Paladin burst across the sky in a trot that would make Pegasus jealous. The HUD inside his helmet lit up, drawing a GPS schematic of the city, with multiple routes leading to Grant Park ten miles away. Two green moving dots—Thief and Blurr—were a good ways between him and the destination. Thief would inevitably get there first, with

Blurr seconds behind. Paladin had quite some ground to make up, but pushing the S3 to the limits in the past paid great dividends as he was able to run down Cheetah-Girl. There was no telling how fast the S4 could perform.

"If you cut across Cabrini Green, you could shave off a little time, Sebastian," Lydia said over the comms.

"Oh, so you want me to get shot on the way to fight a psychopath? I'll pass," Paladin replied.

"Cabrini's cool now. You guys cleared it out a few months ago, remember?"

"I'm good…Go ahead, say it," Paladin teased.

"Say what?"

"Come on. You know what I want to hear."

"What? State the obvious…You'll never catch them at this pace."

Sebastian smiled. "That's what I wanted to hear." The sound of a cannon filled the air as Paladin blazed across the sky, lifting trash and debris from the rooftops of buildings below. Seconds later, he had done the impossible, passing Blurr and landing square in front of Widget Man at the same time as Thief.

"Finally," Thief said.

Paladin shook his head. "Don't try it. I got here right when you did."

"Did not," Thief said.

"Did too."

"Shut up! You two are hilarious," Widget Man said, interrupting.

"But this is my show, my rules, boys."

Blurr landed in between Paladin and Thief. "Rules apply to girls too, Sardine Can?"

"Ooh, the sexy one has arrived. Gang's all here then," Widget Man said. "If my suit is a *can*, then you must be the stale fish that needs confining. Come over. I'm sure I can make room to pack you in."

"That sounds all kinds of gross," Thief said.

"Sorry, pal. That cone-head helmet is a complete turnoff," Blurr said.

"Now, now, now, Wimpy Shades of Grey. That's my girl you're disrespecting. Might want to not do that," Paladin warned, waving a finger.

"Looks like I struck a nerve. Maybe I'll go for two," Widget Man said, pointing his hand at Paladin.

A volley of darts barreled in the group's direction. Thief and Blurr easily dodged them, as the S4's oramite plating surged to three times their original size. The darts pinged off the surface like dead flies as Paladin rested his fists on his hips, chest poked out.

"My turn," Blurr said as he zoomed in close to Widget Man and took a swing at him. The electric force field around him zapped her before she could connect with his face, launching her in the opposite direction. Paladin leaped and snatched Blurr from the air before she could hit the wall of stone behind them.

"Watch those sticky fingers, girly," Widget Man teased.

"How about me, tough guy," Thief said as he moved in to attack.

Thief threw a punch of his own, slipping right through the electric field as his arm turned translucent. His fist solidified as it made contact with Widget Man's mask, right around the area where his jaw would be located. An audible *click* could be heard as his teeth slammed together.

Stunned, Widget Man dropped to one knee as Thief pulled back and watched as the electric force field dissipated. Widget Man shook off the initial sting of the blow and quickly stood, the bumble-bee sized eyes of his mask locking onto Thief's position.

"Sting," Widget Man screamed as a wide spray of darts sailed at Thief once more. This time, Thief was caught off guard; he successfully dodged the darts but ran into the electric field, which was now surrounding both him and Widget Man.

"Ahhhhhh!" Thief yelled as he stood motionless, immobilized by the force of the electric shock.

Widget Man walked over to the Thief and held his hand just inches away from the back of Thief's head. "Don't worry, I'll retrieve my stinger this time."

Before Widget Man could fire again, the ground beneath him exploded, tossing him backward as Blurr burst from the concrete below. The electric force field was interrupted and Thief fell to the floor, dazed. Paladin slipped behind Widget Man in stealth mode and grabbed around the neck. "Yield and we'll call it a draw for today," Paladin said.

Blurr knelt beside Thief. "Are you okay?"

Thief nodded, still stunned by the blast of electricity.

125

Widget Man struggled to break free from Paladin's grasp, half tugging at Paladin's arm and half aiming in Blurr and Thief's direction. "You must let me do this, hero."

"Do what?" Paladin asked.

"The...world...is doomed. The most you can do now...is wipe out the infidels and make way for the new gods," Widget Man said, foregoing any further attempts to pry himself free while aiming at the other two heroes. "I can see the headlines now...'Ex-lovers get stung, But it Ain't by Cupid's Arrow.'"

"Don't do it," Paladin warned, grimacing as he fought to hold back both Widget Man and the rage brought about by his words. The S4's oramite plating slowly inflated to twice its size.

"You...can't...stop...me," Widget Man murmured as Paladin's grip continued to tighten.

"Go to sleep, dammit! I don't want to hurt you," Paladin said.

Widget Man's arms steadied as Paladin watched from behind and noticed Blurr and Thief fit squarely between Widget Man's line of fire. "This is for the best. Beeeeeeeelieveeeee meeeeee," Widget Man said, steadying his aim.

"Noooooooooo!" Paladin screamed, narrowing his grip on Widget Man's neck. The sound of snapping bones rang out as Widget Man's body went limp in Paladin's arms. Paladin loosened his grip and the villain's body crashed to the ground in a pile of lifeless skeleton and muscle.

Blurr stood, silently gazing at Paladin with weak eyes. Paladin stared at his hands as the S4 shrunk to normal size. "Sebas," Blurr cried out, but Paladin wasn't trying to hear it as he jumped into the air and darted off into the distance.

***

Paladin cruised into the penthouse suite as Lydia stood by, arms at her side, quiet. For the first time Paladin could remember, she couldn't find a single word for say.

And how could she? What could she possibly say to console him now? The amount of blood on his hands was rising. Yes, Widget Man was a lunatic, but he thought he had a real chance of helping him.

Paladin snatched off his helmet and tossed it on the couch. Within seconds, the S4 slid from his body and dropped to the floor as Sebastian emerged, visibly troubled, wearing a swath of emotions. He took a seat on the stairs and sunk his head into his hands.

Lydia approached. He could hear her footsteps growing louder and, when she finally came alongside him, the touch of her hand on his shoulder made him flinch. He looked up and watched a stream of tears spill from the corner of her eyes. "Oh, Sebastian," she whispered.

"I couldn't do it, Lydia. I couldn't stop him without killing him."

"I know, Sebas. I know. It's okay."

"That's the problem, though, isn't it? The only way to stop these people is by death alone. There are no alternative methods that work when their minds are so lost."

127

"Sometimes it's just the way things are. Somebody has to make the decisions out there. It has to come from the heroes."

"No," he yelled. "That's just it. I can't continue to go on being judge, jury, and executioner."

"You don't have to be," Blurr said as she raced in through the window. Lydia trailed off as Karla pulled off her hood and knelt next to Sebastian. "You're not out there alone, baby."

"I just don't know if I can keep doing this," Sebastian said.

Karla slipped her hand over his and gave it a firm squeeze. "Yes, you can. Because you have to. That's the burden of wearing the mask. To help those who can't help themselves, even if it means ending them. But I'm here with you, standing beside you. Always."

"You say it as if it's that easy. Aren't you still having second thoughts about protecting these people?"

Karl shook her head slowly. "Not anymore. I learned something from you over these past few weeks, something that hadn't shaken free until now. We live every day of our lives in the hope of the future, but that hope rests squarely on what we do today. You go into each day as if it is the last day and I was so, so obsessed with both my past and future that I didn't take the time to appreciate the tender moments of the *now*. All you do is love me where I am, not where I was or where I will be five or ten years from now. It's a gift you have and I want to try to glean a little bit of that from you now. I want to give myself to you. All of me. You deserve that. If you'll have me."

"Of course, I will," Sebastian said.

Sebastian felt her grip loosen as she slid in closer to his face. "We can only get stronger if we open ourselves up to one another." He closed his eyes as his body drifted in close to her as if awakened by the presence of her soul. His lips pressed into hers and, at once, everything felt right again. Karla pulled back and softly held his face. "You did the right thing out there."

"Then why does it feel so wrong?" Sebastian asked.

"Because if it didn't, you wouldn't be much of a hero, bud," Thief said. He offered a fist to Sebastian, who immediately touched his own fist to it. "It's a conscience that separates us from them."

"Us, huh?" Sebastian asked.

"Yeah, I think I learned a little something from you out there too. You saved my life...again," Thief said with a smile.

"That's two, but who's counting," Sebastian teased.

"B.R.A.I.N., what do we know about our mystery villain?" Thief asked, looking to the ceiling.

"I've analyzed the hair sample you gave me upon your arrival, Alice," B.R.A.I.N. said.

"Seriously?" Thief asked.

Lydia snickered and quickly stopped when Thief shot an angry glare her way. "Sorry."

"You plucked a hair sample from him?" Karla asked.

"The only reason you beat me back here after the fight, darlin'," Thief said.

"Our villain went by the name of Harold Myers, an astrophysicist from the recently decommissioned NASA alien research group," B.R.A.I.N. said.

"I remember reading about that group. Said they were misappropriating funds for private studies. Something about dissecting deceased humans who donated their bodies to science to analyze the effects of deep space radiation and pressure on human anatomy," Lydia chimed.

"Right. But, obviously, they violated about a hundred or more human rights laws by doing so—without the permission of the U.N., no doubt," B.R.A.I.N. added. "Supposedly, Myers was the lead scientist of the group and he became fascinated with deep space alien travel, but it later turned into an obsession. He crossed astrology and astronomy, concluding that there were prophecies of humanity's demise written in monthly horoscopes."

"Doo doo doo doo doo, doo doo doo doo doo," Karla teased.

"The military confiscated his journals during the decommissioning and discovered that Myers was planning a takedown of local government to enact a new militia to allow research of the free world," B.R.A.I.N. said.

"Wait, he was planning a scientific coup?" Sebastian asked.

"Somewhat. Once he was shut down, he lost it and by chance fell into the rainstorm that gave Super-Normals their powers. Or that's what people thought. I did a little digging—no dossiers needed," B.R.A.I.N. said.

"This guy. The A.I. made a funny," Thief said.

"What I found was fascinating. It appears Myers was a close friend of Bernstein and, most likely, the two of them planned the experiment with Myers getting a dose of the treatment," B.R.A.I.N. said.

"But why surface now? Why not join Dark Phase back then?" Lydia asked.

"Fear," Thief said. "He probably lacked the nuts to step to the plate and fight."

"Or he played his role in the background," Lydia added.

"His psychosis evolved along with his powers and he began creating an impressive assortment of prophetic rhetoric depicting the downfall of human civilization," B.R.A.I.N. said.

"Anything to do with pretty meteorites falling from the sky?" Karla asked.

"If you were betting in Vegas, you'd be a billionaire," B.R.A.I.N. said.

"B.R.A.I.N., you got all this information legally, right?"

"Of course, hacked it right from the Pentagon," B.R.A.I.N. said.

Sebastian turned to Lydia. "Cousin?"

Lydia folded her arms. "It's not my fault I made him so generously amazing."

"There is one other thing. The file on Myers noted that his major prophetic babblings centered on the probability of an imminent alien harvest, where humanity becomes food for deep space visitors. Supposedly, it's the reason he snapped and lost his mind."

"He mumbled something to me about that when we were fighting.

Some trash about wiping out infidels and making room for the new gods," Sebastian said.

"Where's that leave Myers? Was he tied somehow to Q-18?" Karla asked.

"Inconclusive at this time," B.R.A.I.N. said.

"We'll never know now," Sebastian said, dejected.

"If it makes you feel any better, Sebastian, I ran the event of Myers' death through multiple high-end predictor protocols and your actions proved to be ninety-nine percent correct," B.R.A.I.N. said.

"Thanks," Sebastian whispered.

Thief broke the Q&A session abruptly. "Let's finish the last bit of packing. We need to get going. I don't like the idea of lingering around here anymore. It's time to get this show on the road. I got an appointment with an oversized diamond."

Sebastian stood. "Good idea. But before we go, I have an appointment of my own. I need to see someone." His eyes beat over to Karla. "And you're coming with me."

Chapter 10

convergence

The tombstone of Sebastian's father stared back at him with an unbelievable heavy silence. Karla held his hand, squeezing softly to get his attention. Sebastian's eyes filled with tears and threatened to overflow, but somehow he managed to keep them from spilling out. "Hey, you. You okay?" she asked.

Sebastian nodded. "Yeah," he muttered.

"Thank you for bringing me here."

"No need to thank me. We can only get stronger if we open ourselves up to one another, right?"

Karla smiled. "Right."

"My father was not a great man."

"But he didn't have to be a great man. He just needed to be your father and, from what you tell me, he wasn't."

"I used to wonder why he didn't do better. You know? Why he was so stuck in the ideals that kept him so isolated like he was stranded in neutral. Not going anywhere on his own and relegated to the action of others to make him move." He looked at Karla. "I vowed I wouldn't be like that...ever."

"And you're not. And you won't be. You have a great heart and that will guide you to always do the right things."

Sebastian knelt at the gravesite and placed two bushels of lilies in

133

the metal planter plunged in the ground in front of the tombstone. Satisfied with their arrangement, he joined Karla again and took her by the hand. He sighed heavily. "It's the first time I've been here since starting my *heroing*. I guess I should say something."

"Yes. He'd like that."

Sebastian gazed at the tombstone. "Hi, Dad. Don't know if you heard the news, but I've decided to take on a new occupation of crimefighting. I, ugh, I'm doing a pretty good job trying to save this city. The mayor gave me a couple of awards for my troubles, and I even got a hot chick by my side." He smiled at Karla. "And now, the United States has asked me and my team to save the world. Pretty cool, huh? Never thought you'd see me do something like that…well, I just wanted to stop by and update you. You always liked to read those superhero comics so, well, I just thought you like to know that your son is finally one of them." Sebastian nervously looked around as if someone were watching.

Karla nudged him. "Intro, please."

"Oh, yeah. Dad, that hot chick is Karla. You may remember her from junior high. Probably not, because I never told you about her. I was kinda scared you'd tell me she was out of my league because, well, truthfully, back then, she was."

"Hello, Mr. Teleford," Karla said, waving.

"Well, that's all. We're going to try to save the world now. Hopefully, I'll be back soon with an update." Sebastian's eyes dropped to the ground, and he turned away. As he and Karla took a couple of steps, they were shocked to see they were not alone.

"Odd," Zenith said, standing alongside a raised tomb.

"Zenith. This is the last place I thought I'd ever see you," Sebastian said.

"Buried or wandering around?" Zenith asked.

"Either, I guess," Sebastian said. "What's so odd about us being here?"

"I pictured the exchange between you and your father to be different," Zenith said.

"How so?" Sebastian asked.

"It seemed so…emotionless," Zenith said.

"What did you expect?" Sebastian snapped.

"More," Zenith said.

"Don't know why someone as powerful as yourself would be so interested in an act as boring and mindless as grave visiting," Sebastian said.

"On occasion, I still mind the ways of Normals from time to time. It keeps me somewhat connected," Zenith said.

"So you were one of us," Sebastian said.

Zenith's eyes widened and burned white-hot. "Tell me, have you calculated all the risks of taking on this…*task* being asked of you?"

"We've played through the scenarios multiple ways," Karla interrupted.

"Ahh, the Conduit speaks," Zenith said.

"Conduit?" Karla asked.

"Yes. You have the gift." Zenith looked at Karla, squinting intently as if searching her thoughts. "You don't know, do you?" He looked over to Sebastian. "I'm surprised you hadn't shared the information with her yet."

"What information?" Sebastian and Karla asked simultaneously.

"The dream, of course," Zenith answered. "You've seen the invasion and the prize."

"What invasion, Sebas?" Karla asked.

"I...I wasn't sure what I was seeing. I just remember seeing you running at super speed and some alien fleet coming to earth and taking you away from me. I...I think I died trying to save you."

"Why didn't you tell me?" Karla asked.

"Because he didn't trust his thoughts," Zenith said. "He had no idea what he was seeing. But that's the power of the Conduit." Zenith pointed at Karla. "You were using him as the vessel to direct the prophetic message from deep space. You've been chosen, Karla. The same entities that speak to Menzuo have reached out to you and the link between you and Sebastian has allowed you to see the future."

Sebastian's hands fisted at his side. "You mean to tell me that aliens are coming and with the intent to take her away?"

Zenith floated from the tomb. "Although the visions are prophetic, they are more metaphorical in nature. In this instance, Karla may represent one thing or multiple things, while the aliens could denote change, resistance to change, or catalysts of change."

"Sounds a little too specific to me. What do you know, Zenith?"

Sebastian asked.

"You know that I cannot interfere," Zenith said.

"Come off of it. That's a load of crap, and you know it. You were once a Normal. A human, for *god's* sake. You are part of the human race whether you like it or not," Sebastian charged.

"I have seen things—great things—from the perspective of both good and bad," Zenith said. "I cannot choose a side. It is not my right or responsibility to. I can only do my best to manage the balance between the two. The Travelers have commanded me to."

"Who are the Travelers?" Karla asked.

"A conversation for another time, perhaps." Zenith closed his eyes momentarily, then opened them. "Actually, yes, another time. I see the exact moment in the future, but it is not now. But I can make the promise that we will have it."

"Sooner or later?" Sebastian asked.

For the first time, a slight smile crept across Zenith's face. "One day. But for now, I need to introduce you to someone."

A dark vortex opened behind Sebastian and Karla, blowing gusts of wind all around them as trash and debris from the graveyard swirled about. Sebastian covered his face with his forearm. "What is it?"

"A gateway to answers," Zenith said above the howling wind.

Karla took Sebastian by the hand and stepped inside. As soon as they entered, the wind immediately stopped. Sebastian looked back through the vortex and noticed that Zenith was still there, sitting in the air with his legs crossed Indian style and his eyes closed. He and Karla were now engulfed in bright light.

A voice rang out, "The Conduit is here." The sound of it was like a sea of crying babies. "Zenith has connected."

"Who are you?" Sebastian asked, gazing into nothingness.

"We are Orchid: purveyors of information."

"Then tell us what we need to know," Karla said.

"The Conduit speaks…the Conduit speaks…the Conduit speaks," the voices repeated.

"Yes, I speak. Help us," Karla said.

The voices rose to the tone of rolling thunder. "You will be Queen one day, as you desire. And the final decision will be yours. But only if you see the smoke on Autumn's veil. If not, hold your time for later."

"More riddles. Give us the truth. What is the sense of us coming here if all we get is more confusion? We need your help," Sebastian said.

"You are the lightning rod. Spare no one in your path," the voices whispered.

Suddenly, the vortex surged and swallowed Sebastian and Karla, bringing them back to the graveyard in front of Zenith. "I'm glad you're back."

"Really? I didn't think you cared," Sebastian said, still screaming as if he was in the vortex.

"I don't. I needed to take a break. That vortex isn't easy to maintain," Zenith said, opening his eyes. "You can stop screaming now."

"Take us back," Karla commanded. "I didn't get all my questions answered."

"That will have to wait. I can only open the vortex every ninety days," Zenith said.

"Why am I not surprised," Sebastian said.

Zenith shook his head. "I'm on your side."

"Could have fooled me," Sebastian said.

"You'll see," Zenith said. "I can, however, answer a few questions. What answers do you seek?"

"Why me?" Karla asked.

"You are a speedster. One who can manipulate windows of time. In this dimension, time has a very strong influence. It controls almost everything we do, who we are, and what we will become. Since speed is a component of time, it makes your skillset a very valuable commodity, as time has a significantly lesser influence on you. As you continue to grow more powerful, less and less time will affect you. Sooner or later, you will see even more visions across the span of the time window. The Travelers have sensed this in you and desire to use you as a medium between dimensions."

"How many dimensions are there?" Sabastian asked.

"Limitless. There used to be a finite number, but as Super-Normals, aliens, and time travel became more prevalent, the rules of the universe have become obsolete."

"Brain-blown," Karla joked.

"Remember everything you heard today. The Orchid speaks

through teleonotioning—conversation without words. Their information has converged with the protein molecules in your brains. You refer to them as memories. They are embedded in your minds forever. You only need the keys to unlock them now. They will lead you when the time is right. No sooner."

"We finally got a time frame out of you," Sebastian said.

Zenith stood and drifted into the sky, looking down on them. "Speaking of time frames, it's 1700 hours. Time for you to get back to your penthouse. The others are waiting for you."

In a burst of light, Zenith disappeared, leaving Sebastian and Karla to trek back alone.

Chapter 11
faults

1800 HOURS

The team regrouped at the penthouse, and Lydia did her best to run through the final checklist of items deemed necessary for the fight. "I've got all the remote equipment I need to establish a connection to B.R.A.I.N.'s core processors here while I run surveillance at the crash site. Other than that, you guys have the latest versions of your suits and the inner earpiece comms are safely tucked away in my bag. I'll hand them out just before the action commences," she said.

"S4 fully charged this time?" Sebastian asked.

"Running at one hundred ten percent, to be exact," Lydia said. "Can't afford to lose any advantages on the field."

"Did Zenith mention any chance of him swinging by the crash site?" Thief asked. "I could use a good drain or two." He pulled his Cowl over his head and gave it a good tug.

"I wouldn't count on it," Sebastian said, holding his helmet underneath his arm.

Karla donned the last glove and fisted her hands to guarantee a good seal. "Well, there's a good chance of us getting our butts waxed so badly out there that he finally decides to intervene and give us a hand or two." She shrugged and drew her speed goggles over her eyes.

"One good chance doesn't guarantee another. Zenith is too detached from humanity now. I don't think he'll ever see things the way we do anymore," Sebastian said, sliding his helmet in place over his head.

"I have to admit, I kinda envy his position. Sometimes I wish I could lose my humanity a bit. You know, forget some of the bad things I've learned. Perhaps a good change of perspective is the one thing humanity needs. We've been somewhat of a brutal beast in our existence," Blurr said.

"Don't start that *detached from humanity* speech nonsense again," Thief warned. "Keeping our humanity is what gives heroes like us the edge. We need it now more than ever."

Paladin gave him an elbow shove. "Look at you. Sounding all heroic and stuff."

"I know. Kinda sexy," Lydia said, biting the side of her lip.

"Stick around. You might see a lot more," Thief teased.

"I like the sound of *that*," Lydia said.

"That's enough," Paladin said. "I can feel the vomit bubbling up my throat from the thought of *it*."

"All right, let's move," Blurr said.

"Wait! We never decided who's the leader here," Lydia said.

The trio slowly looked at one another; each one trying to decide who made the best argument for being dubbed the leader. Blurr shrugged, Thief rolled his eyes, and Paladin nervously rubbed his hands together. When no one spoke up, Lydia chimed in again. "For one, we need a name for the group. I go with The Capes."

"I think we all agree that that sucks," Paladin said.

"Okay, smart guy. You take a stab at it," Lydia said.

"How 'bout Team Storm?" Paladin asked.

"How 'bout that sucks too," Thief said.

"Got a better one?" Paladin asked.

"Crimson Gems," Thief said.

"Vomit rising," Paladin said.

"I've got it," Blurr said, interrupting. "What we are today may not mean a whole lot for the future. I see us getting stronger and bigger as a whole. If we survive this mess, it won't just be us anymore. Others will follow. We have to make this big."

"We're listening," Paladin said.

"Infinity," Blurr said.

Paladin glared over at Thief, reading his face. The name had merit to it, and he didn't need her future-peeking powers to agree that they were all on the verge of something huge.

"If Paladin's in, I'm game," Thief said finally.

Paladin took Blurr by the hand. "I think it's awesome, doll."

"It's still missing something, but it'll do for now," Lydia said. "What about Infinity Capes?"

"Sucks," Paladin, Thief, and Blurr said in unison.

Lydia rolled her eyes. "It'll have to do for now, then. So who's the lead?"

"Blurr thought of the name," Paladin started, squeezing her hand. "So honestly, honey, I elect you."

"I'm cool with it," Thief said.

"It's settled. Let's roll," Lydia said. She looked up at the ceiling. "B.R.A.I.N., you're on deck. Activate all security protocols once we hit the elevator. If anyone trespasses, you know what to do."

"Certainly," B.R.A.I.N. said.

"What does he know to do?" Paladin asked.

Lydia took him by the arm and started to walk him over to the door. "Trust me, you don't want to know. Let's just say I hope you have your homeowners insurance up to date."

***

2100 HOURS

Team Infinity arrived at the pick-up spot—a wide and flat patch of land just outside of Illinois and south of Wisconsin—at the foot of the Charles Mound Mountain. Stars filled the pitch-black night sky.

"Man, from up here, everything seems so close," Lydia said.

"And gorgeous," Blurr said.

"I guess we should set up camp and get settled. We're a little early," Paladin said.

"What do we do with the truck?" Thief asked, looking over at the black Suburban parked along the dusty road.

"We'll take care of it," Captain Terringer said, emerging from the surrounding trees. "Ready to play catch with an asteroid?" Captain Terringer approached Team Infinity, followed by about twenty other soldiers.

144

"Where the hell did you guys come from?" Thief asked.

"We've been here for a while. I'm glad you showed up early. I hate waiting and I'd like to push off as soon as possible," Captain Terringer said.

"You can do me a big favor first and tell me how the hell you have superpowers now," Thief said. "I feel it surging through your body."

Blurr's eyes widened. "Powers? What?"

Captain Terringer smiled proudly, staring at Blurr. "Who did you think was going to lift Q-18 and put it inside the U.S.S. Overdrive?" He turned his sights on Thief. "You're talking about my telekinesis? I used my shielding properties to block you from stealing it from me when we first met at the base. Wasn't sure how you'd act. But, since we're all on the same squad now, I thought I'd drop my guard."

"Well, aren't you full of surprises," Thief said. "Got a call sign?"

"They call me Slingblade," Captain Terringer said. He pointed to his head. "But I don't cut or move objects with physical weapons, only with my mind."

"Nice," Thief said.

"What do you think of the power surging through you?" Captain Terrringer asked.

Thief flexed his arm at his side. A few stones floated from the ground in front of him. "Feels pretty cool to me. Got any more secrets?"

"None worth mentioning," Captain Terringer said.

"What about a suit?" Thief asked.

Captain Terringer gave a thumbs-up gesture. "Of course." Then he looked over to Paladin. "Your team ready?"

Paladin nodded in Blurr's direction. "Uh, you're asking the wrong person. She's the lead."

"You look surprised, Captain. You're not sexist, are you?" Blurr asked, responding to the look on Captain Terringer's face.

"No, not at all. Don't forget, our last president was a woman. I voted for her as well. Welcome aboard," Captain Terringer said, tipping his hat. He pulled out a small device from his pocket and began to peck at the numbers on the front. "I'll call in transport."

Within seconds, the sound of engine noise roared to deafening levels around the team as a large vessel hovered from above the thick trees. Thief and Blurr, lacking the shielding of Paladin's helmet, covered their ears while the rest of Captain Terringer's squad crowded the area, unfazed by the noise. The brown, green, and gray camouflage-colored vehicle was approximately the width of three school buses with equal length, fully equipped with twin rotating engines on either side that swiveled up and down to allow for vertical takeoffs and landings.

"Make room, make room!" one of Captain Terringer's men shouted as the vehicle began to drop from the sky, shifting all kinds of forest debris like loose shrubs, branches, and leaves. When the vehicle settled in safely, the engines cut off and a large door opened from underneath the belly, with a set of stairs leading inside.

"Move, move, move," the same soldier cried as Captain Terringer's entire battalion—some thirty men and women—ran inside.

"Ahh, the Chameleon. The perfect stealth carrier," Captain Terrigner said.

Thief covered his ears. "Did you guys get the memo that stealth means quiet?"

"It purrs when it needs to, Thief. Right now, it's all about growling and making an entrance," Captain Terringer said. "After you, ladies," Captain Terringer said to Blurr and Lydia, giving a slight nod. Lydia and Blurr took him up on his offer and dashed inside, and Thief followed. Paladin lagged, surveying the area curiously. "You're not getting cold feet, are you?" Captain Terringer asked Paladin.

"No, not at all. Just still a little weary, that's all," Paladin said.

"About what?" Captain Terringer asked.

"Mystikal and Mirage. Haven't seen them."

"We had trackers set in place all around the perimeter of the pick-up zone. You guys are fine, trust me."

Paladin gave the most sarcastic smile he could manage, somewhat disappointed that the captain couldn't see it behind his helmet. "On your six, Captain." Captain Terringer walked up the steps and Paladin joined him as they made their way to the large holding bay where the entire crew was camped, sitting side by side facing one another along two rows of cushioned seats with metal harnesses.

Paladin sat beside Blurr, who had saved him a seat, and began to strap himself in. Captain Terringer took his seat across from them, seated next to Lieutenant Dixon. "You hiding any superpowers as well,

Lieutenant?" Paladin asked.

"No. Unless you count my deadly aim. I can shoot a pimple off of a frog's ass," Lieutenant Dixon said, cocking his handgun and loading one in the chamber with a snap.

The troops all erupted in laughter, just the thing to break the suffocating tension forming in the air as the door to the outside world closed. The ship rocketed to the sky just as the sound of the whirling engines screamed. The G-forces were taking a toll on Thief as he slammed his eyelids shut and tightened his grip on his torso harnesses. Lydia was sitting next to him and slipped her hand over his for the next thirty seconds or so until the ship broke through the turbulence of the low hanging clouds.

As things leveled off, Captain Terringer began to debrief Team Infinity. "So we've been able to ascertain the pulse of the rest of the world concerning Q-18 over the last twenty-four hours. From what we gather, about thirty-seven independent counties are tracking its path to Earth and mobilizing teams accordingly. They have small resources and minimal tech to cause a threat, but North Korea, Germany, Canada, and Russia are certainly formidable. We'll be referring to them as the Contenders."

"Never trust the Russians," Thief said, rousing from his momentary nausea. "Any signs of Middle Eastern incursion?"

"Surprisingly, no. I think they've been so entrenched in their own civil unrest with those lunatic dictators that they've passed on getting any of this filthy wealth," Lieutenant Dixon said.

"Not like they need it anyway," Lydia said, still holding onto his hand.

"Has the impact site been compromised yet?" Paladin asked.

"Not yet," Captain Terringer said. "I think that most of the threats want to assure the location of Q-18 makes landfall first before crossing borders. The Navy and Air Force are on high alert for sea and air offensives, but the sheer number they're going to throw at us is too overwhelming to stop. They'll no doubt be able to thin out the basic fleets, but the more advanced technological assets will be our responsibility."

"So how do we run it? Just play Round Robin and pummel countless threats or is there a game plan?" Thief asked.

Lieutenant Dixon looked Captain Terringer's way. "Captain."

Captain Terringer pulled out a large tablet and entered a code on the screen until a 3D model of what was presumably the entire impact site of Q-18 materialized and filled the gap between them. "Our 3D replication of the impact site shows a large twenty-foot zone in the center," he said, pointing in the center, "with that large fault line trailing another hundred feet to the left. If you look closely, there are two other small fault lines along the front and left side of the crater. Those are faults one and two and measure about thirty feet each. They represent some trenching that we've already manually prepared to help our troops set up a foothold to fight off invaders. That large one in the back is the fault line of where we predict Q-18 will slide once it hits the ground. NASA already has the cooling foam on site. Once Q-18 comes to a halt, we'll slather that bad boy up with foam and then the games will begin."

Lieutenant Dixon cut in. "The heroes—"

"Team Infinity," Blurr said, interrupting.

"Team Infinity?" Lieutenant Dixon asked.

"Yes. That's our squad," Blurr clarified.

"Nice," Lieutenant Dixon said with a slight smile. "Team Infinity will form a wall about halfway between the impact site and the final resting place of Q-18."

"Off to the side, you'll notice two small huts," Captain Terringer said. "The larger one houses the U.S.S. Overdrive and the smaller is where Lydia will set up to assist in coordinating your efforts."

"Aww, you did think of us," Lydia said.

"Wouldn't be much of a plan if we didn't do our homework. We know how you guys operate and we want it to go as smoothly as possible," Lieutenant Dixon said, winking.

"This will be a success, folks. It has to be," Captain Terringer said.

"Looks like you thought of *everything*," Thief said.

"You don't sound convinced," Captain Terringer said.

"Been around long enough to know one thing about war. Account for everything, *Captain*," Thief said.

Captain Terringer opened his hand and the tablet levitated before shutting off and floating back into his hand. He slid it down into his satchel beside him. "Good advice."

"We've got a good seven hours before we make it to the impact site. Q-18 should be on our short-range sensors two to three hours after that and so should the Contenders. I suggest everyone get some shut-eye. Won't have much time to get it in later," Lieutenant Dixon said.

"Or you can feel free to stretch your legs a bit. We've passed the turbulence, so everyone can walk around," Captain Terringer said.

Lieutenant Dixon loosened his harness and stood. "Captain, a word please."

Captain Terringer stood and followed Lieutenant Dixon into another section of the ship, away from the others.

"Uh oh. Military mind huddle up. Normally means this is the moment we get shunted into the *Need to Know* group," Thief said.

"Yeah, I was wondering when it'd happen. They've been way too transparent," Paladin said.

"Maybe they just see that this is too important to hide secrets now. The fate of the world is at stake," Lydia said.

"Lydia, Lydia, Lydia," Paladin said. "The world is always at stake. The United States knows how to play spy better than anyone else on the planet."

"To be honest, I'd be panicking a bit if they didn't follow their usual script," Blurr said.

"Exactly. Everyone's got to be on their A-game if we have a chance," Thief said.

Blurr turned to Paladin and placed her hand on top of his. "How you holding up?" she whispered.

"Honestly?" Paladin asked.

"Of course. The only way I'd take it," Blurr said.

"I'm still kinda anxious over the idea of killing again. I know it's gonna happen here. There are too many numbers," Paladin said.

"Well, how do you plan to get around it?" Blurr asked.

"I haven't quite figured that out yet."

"Don't worry, I'm here with you."

"I know. But I don't want to jeopardize the mission or the chance that you may get hurt. I'm only out there to protect you."

"That type of talk is going to get you killed. You've got to block me out. I'm a big girl. I can take care of myself."

"I know, I know," Paladin said.

"I'd hate to think that I'm a distraction for you. You have to block out your feelings for me on the battlefield, Sebas," Blurr whispered.

"I know...and I will. It's just hard," Paladin said.

Blurr sighed. "Well, let's make a pact. I promise to not kill anyone—Normals only—if you promise to keep your head on a swivel and keep safe. I don't want to lose you, either."

"Deal. Plan on doing a little overdriving of your own, huh?"

"You can say that," Blurr said with a wink.

"But how do you plan on fighting and not killing?" Paladin asked.

Blurr scissored her fingers. They moved faster and faster until Paladin could no longer see them at all. "Speed, baby. Speed kills. But not like you think in this case. I plan on setting some new records out there. If I travel fast enough, I might be able to slip in and out of time, foreseeing death before it comes. I can manipulate actions—at least for myself—in a way that I can make non-lethal takedowns. You can do the same. Use a mix of your stealth and strength to block, parry, and evade. You can disable the Contenders' weapons."

Paladin nodded. Her plan had merit, but there was a catch to following it. For him to be as sharp as she desired, he'd have to forgo his love for her—and that was something that he just couldn't bring himself to do. Deep down inside, he couldn't one hundred percent commit to what she was asking him to do, and completely ignoring her on the battlefield was out of the question. But he wouldn't let her know that. "Perfect. I'm game."

Blurr leaned in close and snuggled her head into his shoulder, firmly clutching his arm. "I love you so much."

Paladin rubbed her head with his free hand. "I know, doll baby. I love you too."

Chapter 12
Three minutes and counting

8 HOURS LATER

The Chameleon settled into a small landing zone just outside of the impact site. The snow beneath the vessel instantly melted as heat from the pair of twin jets scorched the ground. The aft door opened and, as the stairs lowered, troops emptied from the vessel with absolute precision, heading straight to their respective stations.

Team Infinity followed close behind Captain Terringer and Lieutenant Dixon as not to get lost. The base camp was an impressive sight to behold, offering multiple makeshift shelters for weapons, communications, and supplies. The forward bunker was large, sporting a snow-covered camouflage cover with a large, white net to blend in with the surroundings. Large assortments of military men and women scrambled around like busy worker-ants doing god knows what, but the unwavering display of diligence gave the entire Infinity team a much-needed dose of relief.

Captain Terringer and Lieutenant Dixon led the team over into the forward bunker and ushered them inside. The room was no bigger than your average school classroom, but the wall to wall buzzing computers made Lydia feel right at home. "Oh my. Semi-conductors and geo-storm calculators. This is next, next-level stuff," she said, touching a nearby console.

"Did you expect any different, ma'am?" Lieutenant Dixon asked.

"Not at all. Is this where I'll be setting up?" Lydia asked.

"Actually, we're going to give you a bird's-eye view from the Chameleon. You'll be in the spy nest on the top of the ship," Lieutenant Dixon said.

"Oh, okay. I didn't see anything like that," Lydia said.

"We didn't show it to you. But, rest assured, you'll be perfectly safe and have all the resources you'll need," Lieutenant Dixon said. "It's protocol to keep Civi's out of harm's way."

"Roger that," Lydia said.

An ensign sat in front of a long table equipped with an oversized digital board littered with multiple keys, switches, and dials. Just in front of him was a large screen—about eight feet wide—divided into four quadrants. The ensign wore a headset with a small mic protruding from it. Captain Terringer approached him. "Sitrep, Ensign."

"Multiple—and I mean multiple—bogeys have entered into the Soft Zone, converging on approach to the Hard-Line, sir," Ensign Donner said.

"What's the Soft Zone and the Hard-Line?" Paladin asked.

Captain Terringer tapped a button on the console and the entire screen flickered on, displaying an overhead view of the South Pole with the impact site in the center. Three circles rippled out from the middle in colors of red, then green, and finally blue. Numerous triangles in varying bunches from all directions pulsed on and off as they advanced toward the center. "Those red triangles are all of our diverging Contenders. The blue circle was the Outer Zone. Notice that

155

they've already crossed that border and are now piercing the green one. That's the Soft Zone. Once they hit the red one, the Hard-Line, it's—"

"On like Donkey Kong," Paladin chimed.

"How long before they penetrate the Hard-Line?" Lieutenant Dixon asked.

"We're a little ahead of schedule, sir. Projections of Q-18 touching down are between one to two hours from now, and we expect Hard-Line penetration in approximately one hour," Ensign Donner said.

"That gives the Contenders exactly twenty minutes to reach us," Lieutenant Dixon said.

"How many Contenders are confirmed so far?" Paladin asked.

"Twenty Independents and three heavyweights: Russia, North Korea, and Germany. Canada backed out," Lieutenant Dixon said.

"No help from the UK or France?" Paladin asked.

"They're here. Lent their naval vessels and aircraft. We'll hear the booms of cannon fodder soon. The sky will light up the biggest, baddest Fourth of July fireworks display ever," Captain Terringer said.

"Ahh, it'll be so pretty from up top," Lydia said.

"Seriously, cousin?" Paladin asked.

"It all mixes for one hell of a party," Thief said rather emphatically.

"How's that a party," Blurr said, eyebrow raised.

Captain Terringer turned to Lydia. "Time to get you set up. I'll have one of my men escort you to the Chameleon."

Paladin took Lydia by the arm. "Don't do anything crazy out there."

"I was just about to say the same thing to you, cousin," Lydia said.

"I'm serious. We're the heroes, not you. I can't…lose you," Paladin said, choking up.

Lydia smothered him with the biggest hug he ever felt her give, so much so that he swore it'd break his ribs if not for the oramite plating. "Do your job and you won't." He could hear the fear in her voice as it trembled.

She pulled back and blew him a kiss. Blurr hug her as well and kissed her forehead. Thief offered her a handshake, but she was way too emotionally charged now to accept that, opting instead to plant a heavy kiss on his lips and hang on tightly until a soldier appeared and tapped her on the shoulder.

"Time to go, ma'am," the soldier said.

Lydia shooed him away as Thief stood still, allowing her to remain locked to his lips.

"Ma'am, it's time," the soldier repeated.

Paladin and Blurr snickered, more at the expression of discomfort on Thief's face than anything else.

The soldier tried one more time. "Ma'am—"

"All right already," Lydia screamed, wiping her lips. "You think a girl can grab one last kiss before the world implodes on itself." Her eyes beat to Thief. "I'm sorry, Alice, I mean, Thief."

"Don't be. I'm divorced now. We can talk later. *After* we kick these claim-jumper's collective asses," Thief said, smiling.

Lydia's eyes bulged. "Well, all the hell right then! I'll be back." Lydia held her arm out to the soldier, who uncomfortably hooked his arm around hers and escorted her out. "Toodles," Lydia chirped over her shoulder.

Paladin folded his arms across his chest and closed in on Thief. "So, Lydia huh?"

"You...don't approve, I take it," Thief said.

Paladin shook his head. "Hell, it's the end of the world, right? I was waiting for Hell to freeze over, but this is as good a sign as any, I guess."

"If you would excuse me, everyone, I need to go change," Captain Terringer said.

Lieutenant Dixon waved the team over. "Final debriefing, everyone." As they crowded around him, Ensign Donner clicked away at the console, refreshing the screen with new images as appropriate. "We've got movement from all directions. It's going to get crazy really fast. Once Q-18 touches down, wait until it comes to a stop and measure the distance between the front line and its final resting place. There's four of you, counting Slingblade, so that'll allow for a four corners, diamond-shaped formation, isolating Q-18 in between all of you. Your backs should be facing it." He held his hand out to them. "Lydia gave me these earlier. This will give you direct contact between one another, Lydia, and our forward bunker. We'll be able to update trajectories of incoming Contenders so that you can triangulate the best angle of attack to defend the scientists cooling Q-18." They each took an inner earpiece comm and inserted it in their ears. Paladin slid open a small panel along the side of his helmet and replaced the old one with the new modified version. "Remember, we only need three minutes."

"I'll pass on the low hanging fruit that is pointing out that ridiculous time window," Thief said.

"Well, technically you just didn't," Paladin said.

"Oh, right," Thief said, flashing a sarcastic smile.

"Once Q-18 is cooled, Slingblade will move it into the U.S.S. Overdrive for extraction. It will be coming from the south of the impact crater. We have to keep it hidden as long as possible. Any questions?" Lieutenant Dixon asked.

"We're good," Blurr said.

"All right then." Lieutenant Dixon looked down at his watch. "We have about another hour and a half before showtime. You're more than welcome to stay here until then. I will come and get you shortly."

***

Team Infinity held a position of about a hundred yards behind the forward bunker, awaiting the signal from Lieutenant Dixon to broadcast across the comms. The sky had already begun to light up with hues of yellow bullet rounds, as orange, red, and black clouds burst across the sky, signifying the advancing Contenders and Independents. The sound of cannon fire cracked the silence of the once tranquil snow-covered grounds, although most of the snow in the vicinity had all but vanished, successfully cleared away by the U.S. and allied soldiers.

"The strategy is clear. Play defense, not offense, guys," Blurr said across the comms. "Don't chase anyone!"

"Right," Paladin and Thief said in unison.

If the forward bunker represented the north position, then Blurr held the tip of the diamond-shaped formation, with Thief positioned east, Paladin in the west, and Slingblade completing the south. Not much fanfare was paid to Slingblade's suit since it was more of an alpha version of Team Infinity's at best, resembling more military than anything Super-Normal. The torso portion of his bodysuit was all brown, hugging his skin closely and showing off his surprisingly ripped physique while his pants sported a military-fatigue color pattern of light blue, gray, and black, with patches of brown to complement his boots and forearm-length gloves. But his silver mask was the biggest joke, covering his eyes and nose, wrapping around the back of his head and dropping off the front of his face in the shape of a hooked blade. Paladin wondered if he'd ever tried to impale an enemy with it, but decided to save those questions for later. He did, however, make a mental note to upgrade the captain as soon as possible if they all survived, with a possible invitation to join their squad if he was able to hold his own.

"Enemies engaging…forces depleting…holding on coordinates 5 Delta, 3 Charlie, and 9 Echo. Stay frosty, we've got company from the south," Ensign Donner said.

"I've got them," Slingblade said, jumping into action. Slingblade pummeled a pair of jeeps with a supersonic sound blast that flipped them back into the air about fifty feet. A dozen foot soldiers weaved around the exploding vehicles and opened fire on him. Slingblade erected a sonic wall between them that repelled the bullets back at the soldier, wounding half of them.

"They're early," Blurr said.

"Actually, they're not. Q-18 is on its way, and it's a beauty," Lydia said, watching above from the Chameleon.

Team Infinity watched the sky as it changed from bright yellow to dark gray and then smoldering black. Seconds later, it evolved into a large ball of shimmering jewels encased in a blazing, angry, red fire. Paladin changed the filter on his HUD to dim the light just enough to track it while Thief and Blurr moved aside and looked in the opposite direction, avoiding any risk of being blinded by its brilliance.

Q-18 slammed into the ground and shook the earth for what felt like an eternity. Anything not nailed down tumbled over, except the forward bunker, which had been secured by steel gratings and stakes. Even Paladin, Thief, and Blurr fell backward from the force. Q-18 dredged a large fissure the width of a basketball court from the heat of his magnificent wake, although the asteroid itself was only half the size of a compact car. Steam, ash, and embers singed the ground.

"That's the last of them back here. They ran away. I think it was Vietnam," Slingblade said.

Lieutenant Dixon smiled. "You cleared the way. Scientists moving into position. Set your clocks, folks. Three minutes and counting,"

Chapter 13
CLASH

Fighter jets streaked across the sky, dispersing the black cloud of ash trailing from the downed asteroid, followed by Gatling gun rounds and missile fire. Ships dropped from the sky and exploded against the tundra as tanks, Jeeps, and motorcycles pressed their attack. Ensign Donner railed off updates on how well allied forces were holding up against the onslaught as Team Infinity partook in the action.

Blurr took point, zipping in and around attacking vehicles, lifting many of them off the ground by the strength of her speed wake. As oncoming soldiers desperately fired bullets at her, she batted bullets back at them, careful to aim at their knees, elbows, and wrists—crippling but not killing. As she sped by others, she casually slapped them across the back of their necks, knocking them out cold. Any weapons unhinged from the soldiers were broken in half by either well-timed kicks or karate chops.

Paladin kept an eye on Blurr at a distance, awaiting the oncoming troops to engage from the horizon as they closed in. As a tank opened fire, the projectile exploded against Paladin's chest, tickling his pectoral muscles underneath, forcing him to chuckle a little. The strength variant of the S4 was unfazed, as the oramite swelled to reinforce his armor plating. Troops opened fire on him, pelting his body with round after round of bullets, none of which made a single dent on him. It was more annoying than anything, as the streams of warheads clouded his vision, making it difficult to see. Paladin extended his hand and covered his face to take in the rest of the invaders. Swarms of military troops swooped in, making the mistake of testing their fate with hand to hand combat. Paladin swatted them away like flies, tossing them some twenty to thirty feet in the air with a flick of his wrist.

A Jeep slammed into Paladin and folded around his body like melted plastic. He peeled himself free and tossed the useless vehicle at another oncoming tank, blocking the driver's sights. As the tank passed by Paladin, he grabbed it from behind and lifted it with one hand before aiming it at another tank. But this time, instead of hitting the other vehicle, he plunged it into the ground, making a ramp that launched the oncoming tank into a somersault and an upside-down landing.

Thief got into the action as well, phasing in and out of sight while passing into tanks, Jeeps, and helicopter and tossing the pilots and drivers out of them. As a foot soldier tossed a grenade at him, Thief snatched it from the sky, jumped inside a tank, and phased back out before it exploded. Another foot soldier fired a bazooka at him. Thief used his newly acquired telekinesis power to disassemble the entire warhead and drop it to the ground two feet away from him.

"I like this," Thief said, admiring his handiwork.

Two Russian Migs passed overhead and Thief clapped his hands in their direction, forcing the rockets to implode and fall right out of the sky. He noticed a lone motorcycle breaking through the blockade and heading toward the scientists, so he stole a little speed from Blurr and ran after him. Before the Kamikaze cyclist could get any closer, Thief phased inside his body and took over the motorcycle, turning it back into the direction of a troop of soldiers. Thief jumped off the motorcycle, ripped it into pieces, and impaled each one of the soldiers with a part from the motor. Thief looked at his hands and feet, realizing that he was still in the driver's body. Thief spun in a circle at super speed, ripping the flesh from the soldier's body until nothing remained.

Thief dusted his hands free and looked over at Slingblade, watching his six. Slingblade was holding his own, shooting sonic beams from his eyes, incinerating soldiers in seconds, and exploding ATVs, cars, and tanks at ease.

"I've got German forces rallying at noon, Blurr!" Lydia screamed.

Blurr used her super-speed to ram into armored personnel carriers, turning them on their sides and dislodging troops from their bellies. She ran in circles, creating a thirty-foot dust cloud wall that sent the men scurrying.

Paladin went into stealth mode next, momentarily turning invisible so that he could flank more advancing troops and then switching back and forth between stealth and strength to topple the unsuspecting soldiers like bowling pins. "This is like child's play," Paladin said. "How you guys holding up?"

"I'm fine. Just falling in love with myself all over again. This telekinesis, speed, and phasing combo is crucial. These Normals don't stand a chance," Thief said, gloating.

"One and a half minutes left," Ensign Donner said.

The team of Capes fought desperately to hold off droves on incoming armies, repelling hundreds of foot soldiers and vehicles at a time. The concept of success was very subjective at this point as there was seemingly no end to the onslaught before them, but somehow, each one of them had survived up to this point.

"Uh oh. Something just appeared on the radar," Lydia said. "And it's moving fast."

"Ahh, geez. Just when things were going well," Paladin said.

"I see it. Clear out, guys!" Ensign Donner said just as the sound of static rang out over the comms.

"Donner!" Lydia yelled.

Paladin looked over to the forward bunker, flattened by a new Super-Normal resembling a large red gorilla, but more manly. "Is that what I think it is?"

"I think so," Thief said, coming alongside him.

The beast stood about nine feet tall and its arms dragged along the ground. "That looks like Gertha from the Chicago Zoo. I heard rumors that she died shortly after the storm."

"Well, she ain't dead, mate," Thief said, pointing as the beast began to beat her chest. "And she looks mean as hell."

"But how did it get over here?" Paladin asked.

"I ain't ever known a gorilla to need fine jewelry," Blurr said. "You guys take it out. I'll help Slingblade keep the others off the scientists."

Before Paladin could move, the beast was upon him and double punched him in the chest. The blow sent Paladin flying across the ground, tumbling back about fifty feet.

"Bastard," Thief said, phasing out of sight before the beast could connect on another blow. Thief materialized again and tried to kick it in the back of the head. But the beast was incredibly fast, blocking the attack with lightning speed and backhanding Thief in the face. The blow knocked Thief to the floor, but before he could attempt to stand, the beast snatched him from the ground and began to spin him around in a circle. Thief phased out again and slipped between the beast's fingers. The beast lost his footing and fell over backward.

Paladin changed variants, switching to speed. "I didn't say anything about not killing *animals* today." He jetted after the beast and connected three blows to his face. The beast screamed so loud that it incapacitated Paladin, making him cover his ears and disorienting him. Instinctively, he knew what was coming next and switched back to strength, swelling to the exact size as the beast. The beast launched itself on Paladin, attempting to twist the helmet from his body. Paladin grabbed his helmet and fought to keep it on, but he was no match for the creature's incredible strength, slowly losing the battle as the helmet lifted inches at a time.

"Thirty seconds left," Lydia warned.

The weight of the beast began to lighten as a small telekinetic shield formed around Paladin, prying the beast from his body. Paladin sailed across the battlefield in the direction of Blurr. "What the hell," he whispered. A telekinetic wall formed behind him. When he looked back, Thief was on the other side of the wall, engaging the beast all by himself, phasing in and out of focus, moving at lightning speed, and forming small, telekinetic shields around his body to block any attacks from the beast. "No!" Paladin screamed.

"Another, incoming," Lydia screamed. "Underneath you!"

The ground beneath Team Infinity erupted as a solo humanoid emerged, floating inside a lightning bubble. "It can't be," Blurr said.

Dame Lightning laughed maniacally. "I'm baccckkk. And better than ever."

She tossed three lighting rays at Blurr, but Paladin got between them and absorbed them, sending an electric surge through his helmet and shorting out the NAV and HUD systems. "Damnit! I'm virtually blind."

"Blind!" Blurr screamed.

"I can see, just not…all fancy-like," Paladin said.

Slingblade attacked Dame Lightning, pelting her with volley after volley of telekinetic bolts, which did not affect her lightning shield. The more he attacked, the more she laughed. "Dowwwwmnnnnnnn, boooooooyyyyyyyy," Dame Lightning sang, raining lightning bolts down on Slingblade. If not for the protection of his telekinetic shield, he would have been incinerated instantly. Still, the electricity took a toll on his body, sending him into a series of convulsions that dropped him from the sky like a dead fly. Paladin activated his strength variant and launched himself Slingblade's way, catching him in the air before he could hit the ground. Paladin bounded once more and took Slingblade to safety in the perimeter where the U.S.S. Overdrive was safely tucked away. He handed him over to one of the soldiers keeping watch. "Look after him. I'll be back."

***

"Down boy, down boy," Thief said, taking jabs at the beast in his best attempt to beat him into submission. But the rage inside the animal was relentless, and each swing Thief took only made her more ravenous. The beast had now grown at least two feet taller since the fight began and equally more massive in width. Thief had a difficult time keeping up with her, as more and more of the beast's attacks broke through the shields and connected with Thief's torso, leaving scratches along his skin.

***

Blurr was working her magic on the battlefield, easily phasing between time intervals of future and present. She could see everything as if it were happening in slow motion. If someone was trying to shoot at her, she'd anticipate exactly where the shot was coming from, move to that location ahead of time and then free the soldier from the weapon before they could even cock it. But, as well as her body was handling the transitions, her mind couldn't keep up. She began to have delusions with past, present, and future all intertwining at once. She couldn't decipher real from fake anymore and began to attack everything in sight—even if it wasn't really there. "Come on, I'll take all of you!"

"Paladin, Blurr needs you. She's doing something weird," Lydia said.

Paladin returned to the battlefield. "Where is she?"

"To your six. She's drifting in and out of time, screaming out loud as she fights. But no one is there."

Paladin scanned the horizon and finally saw what Lydia was describing. He changed into his speed variant and quickly ran to the last place he saw her. But she wasn't there. Every time she flickered into existence, she disappeared just as fast. Paladin couldn't keep up, no matter how hard he tried.

"The scientists are under attack," Lydia said.

"How many Contenders are left?" Paladin asked.

"B.R.A.I.N. says that ninety percent of the Contenders have been wiped out and all Independents have fled," Lydia said. Suddenly, she screamed, "Oh, no! Sebastian!"

Paladin's eyes immediately darted to the sky, watching as the Chameleon appeared, its high tech active camouflage disrupted by Dame Lightning's electric blasts. Explosions ripped from the twin-engines as the ship tilted and began to spiral to the surface.

"Nooooooo," Paladin screamed. For the first time since entering the battle, time stood still. Thief, the scientists, Slingblade, Lydia, and Blurr were all on the verge of death—and he had to choose. *I can't save all of them*, he thought.

An image of Blurr filled his gaze. "You can't save me. I told you not to be distracted," she said.

"I can't…I can't leave you, Karla," he said.

"You promised, Sebas. And you have to keep your promise."

"No. I can't, Karla. I can't."

"If you truly love me, Sebas, you'd maintain my trust. Help the others."

"Karla, please don't make me do it. Don't make me choose."

Blurr's image slowly faded, and time began to speed up to real-time again. But this time, Thief's close-quarters fight with the beast and the sputtering Chameleon just seconds away from crashing came to view. *Speed kills*, he recalled Blurr saying earlier. He had one shot and he had to make good on it.

Paladin switched to his speed variant and exploded into full throttle. He rammed his body into the beast. The creature was no match for the force of the oramite plating against its flesh, and the animal burst into flames. Keeping the same momentum, Paladin grabbed Thief by the arm and spun on one foot, hurling Thief toward the Chameleon. Thief caught onto the plan and phased out of sight just as he entered the ship, grabbed Lydia, phased back out, and exited on the other side just before it hit the ground and exploded. Thief formed a telekinetic shield around Lydia and laid her body—unconscious from the dreadful experience—on the ground.

Dame Lightning turned her focus on Q-18. "I think I'll take my stone now. You know what they say, diamonds are a girl's—"

"You're no girl, Dame," Zenith said, drifting between Dame Lightning and Q-18.

"Zenith," Paladin said in awe.

Zenith raised a hand and encased Dame Lightning inside a net of pure crystal that began to close in on her. "But you can have all the sparkles you want."

Dame Lightning screamed as the crystal netting cut into her flesh and sliced her into thousands of pieces until nothing was left. Blood poured to the ground below. Zenith looked over at Paladin and his eyes burned white. He opened his hand and a vortex appeared. "Retrieve the Conduit."

Paladin ran inside the vortex and quickly returned, carrying Blurr in his arms. He knelt and looked up at Zenith. "Thank you." Zenith nodded and vanished.

Thief came alongside Paladin. "Is she all right?"

"I think so," Paladin said, clearing the hair from her face.

"Take care of her. I'll take care of *this*, bud," Thief said. He ran full speed toward Q-18 and used his telekinesis to lift the cooled asteroid from the rubble. Slingblade had recovered from his convulsions and cleared out the rest of the Contenders from the vicinity. "Take it to the ship."

The U.S.S. Overdrive hovered some ten feet above the ground with its back door open. Thief placed Q-18 inside the cargo hold. He looked over to Slingblade. "Who's driving it?"

Slingblade pulled out a tablet and pressed a few buttons. "It's automated." The back door of the U.S.S. Overdrive closed just as it rocketed into the sky. Seconds later, the ship broke orbit becoming a mere flicker in the empty blackness. Slingblade tapped the tablet once more and a dazzling explosion filled the sky.

"It's the most beautiful thing I've ever seen," Thief said.

Chapter 14
reflections

The smoldering battlefield glimmered, reflecting the stars of the night as the water from the melting snow began to freeze from the frigid temperature. Paladin was sitting along the side of an ambulance, holding an oxygen mask to Blurr's mouth and keeping her close to his chest, trying desperately to keep her warm. It was all he could do to will her back to the present. For all he could ascertain, she was alive, but not well. She was breathing, but fast asleep and periodically twitching as if trapped in a nightmare of some kind.

Thief had moved into detective mode, rounding up what little bits of evidence remained of the fight with the intent of preparing for future engagements. He had directed another ensign to do the diligence of collecting samples from the two Super-Normals and fragments from the crater left behind by Q-18.

"Here you are, sir," the ensign said, handing over a black leather satchel.

Thief looked inside and eyed the contents carefully. Two mason jars labeled "Super Samples" and three Yeti cups filled the bag. It was a poor man's evidence kit, but it would have to do for now. "They're all sealed. Good job."

The ensign walled off, and Thief tossed the satchel over his shoulder and joined Paladin. "How's she doing?" he asked.

"Still breathing, still here," Paladin said.

"Lydia's in recovery at the Medic tent. She's looking for you. But, don't worry, I told her you were with Blurr."

"Thanks." Paladin looked down at Blurr's face. "I just don't know why she's still not waking up."

"Wherever she was, Zenith helped you find her for a reason. That's all that matters. It must mean something."

"Zenith...yeah. He really showed up today," Paladin said, sounding slightly amazed.

"And he doesn't do that. Not for anyone. Things must be a lot worse than I initially thought if he's intervening."

"Dame Lightning's return from the dead, the crazy beast. All of them came from Hero City to do what? Collect some lavish asteroid. What do you think it all means?"

Thief lifted the satchel from his back and held it up at eye level. "Don't know, but I'm guessing the answers are all right here. Nice throwback there, by the way."

"Thanks," Paladin said.

Blurr began to rouse from her slumber and Paladin shifted to give her room to sit up. "What happened to me?" she asked.

"Do you remember anything?" Paladin asked.

Blurr held her head. "The last thing I recall was running around the battlefield, trying to stop everyone. I felt like my body was splitting into multiple directions. It was like I was one hundred percent in the past, present, and future—all at once."

"Well, you made it back and that's all that matters now. We'll sort out all the details later," Paladin said.

Blurr looked around, surveying the area. "So we're all in one piece. I guess that means we won."

"Hopefully," Thief interjected. "We'll take the day to recover and then start trying to piece everything together. Something tells me a lot is going on underneath the surface."

Slingblade joined the group. "How you feeling, Blurr? You gave us all a good scare."

"Better, thanks," she said.

"You should talk. How are *you* feeling?" Thief asked.

"You know, I think all that stimulation woke up my muscles a bit. I think I can go a few more rounds if anyone's game. Just getting my second wind," Slingblade said.

"Right. Right after Dame Lightning knocked the first one out of you," Thief said.

"Touché," Slingblade said.

"So we kept our end of the bargain. What's next for the United States? Will they do what they promised?" Paladin asked.

Slingblade flashed the screen of his tablet at Paladin. An image of his bank account was there with a deposit slip amount of ten million dollars. "They made a very generous donation to your account, Sebastian. All you have to do is make sure it gets to the right people of Chicago."

"You trust me that much, huh?" Paladin teased.

"They trusted you with a Quintillion. Figure they could give you a cool couple of million to weigh down your pockets for a while. You'll do right by your city, I'm sure," Slingblade said.

"Any update on the world militaries?" Blurr asked.

"For the most part, everyone has returned to their respective corners. The loss of such a big haul is somewhat discouraging to most of them. A lot of the Independents invested everything they had into securing the asset. It'll be a long time before they recover from it. Maybe this will be a moratorium on war for a while," Slingblade said.

"What's next for you, hero?" Thief asked Slingblade.

"I'm not sure. This was my first time really using my powers to fight and, I gotta say, it was pretty cool," Slingblade said.

Paladin offered Slingblade his hand. "Well, if you ever want to join up—"

"Don't worry. I know where to find you," Slingblade said.

***

ONE WEEK LATER

The Beacon was bustling with traffic. Lydia had successfully recovered from her injuries and was busy running the joint as Sebastian had expected, coordinating housekeepers and kitchen staff to prepare their new home for the much- deserved housewarming party.

"Bring all the vases over here and then make sure all the tables are lined up without any gaping. We don't want the wine glasses to slip through the cracks," Lydia said, speaking to a Hispanic woman wearing a black apron and a white dress.

"Yes, Miss Lydia," the woman replied.

Sebastian stood off to the side, leaning against the wall, observing her handiwork. "Slave driver," he joked.

Lydia turned to him, narrowed her eyes, and approached, waving her finger at him. "Don't try it. It isn't every day that the mayor graces your home with her presence, Sebas. Every big wig in the city will be here in less than five hours. I just want everything to look wonderful."

Sebastian laughed and cupped her shoulders. "You don't have to worry about a thing. I'm sure it will all be wonderful, cousin."

"How you settling in?" Lydia asked.

Sebastian looked around. The interior of the Beacon was quite a stunner. Immaculate floors, walls, and windows dazzled at every square foot. The thirty-foot ceilings and six-inch crown molding was a sight to behold along with multiple knock-off famous paintings and statues straight from the pages of *The Odyssey* or Shakespeare. "It's not home, but it's starting to rub off on me. How 'bout you?"

"Not so bad. It'll work, I guess."

Sebastian waved her off. "Whatever. You know it's pretty fly. How's B.R.A.I.N. liking it?"

"It was a little weird at first. You know, having access to so much power. But once I was able to upload him to the mainframe and he had a chance to familiarize himself with the CPU, he eased in quite nicely."

"Give him and yourself some time. We just moved in a couple of days ago."

"I'll sleep a little easier when I know we've found Mystikal and Mirage."

"True. But the Feds promised me that they cleaned this place from top to bottom. No bugs or tracers present."

"I saw that you had the new Perfect Safe security system installed. They use some next level NASA-type encryption. Wasn't that expensive?"

Sebastian smiled. "Uh, I know a guy."

"Zenith, right. You guys all buddy-buddy now?"

"Let's just say he owes me one and I owe him about…" Sebastian paused as Karla entered the room wearing a yellow flowy sundress and a pair of three-inch heels. Her hair was in a top knot and the black eyeshadow accented her eyes perfectly, making her resemble a Greek goddess. "A million bucks," Sebastian finished.

Karla walked over and kissed him. "You approve, I take it?"

"Do I!" Sebastian said.

"Ah, you're stunning," Lydia said.

"Thank you," Karla said. "How're the arrangements going?"

"Don't get me started," Lydia said. She looked over at a couple of ladies who were debating on where to place the centerpieces. "Hey, hey, hey. I said over there. You have to work from the center, then out." Lydia threw her hands up and walked over to them, leaving Sebastian and Karla alone.

"So, handsome, what's next on the agenda?" Karla asked.

"Whatever do you mean," Sebastian replied.

"You were up all night tinkering on that new super computer of yours. I didn't hear you come to bed."

"I was just surfing the web."

"I've been with you all this time and you still don't know that I know when you're lying. Spit it out."

"All right, you got me. I was reviewing some information that Thief sent me."

"Let me guess, more secret *dossiers*?"

"Right."

"Anything of interest?"

Sebastian sighed. "He was looking into the Travelers and trying to link it to those red spores we found on the remnants of Caine. Oddly, he found traces of those same spores in the tissue samples from the beast and Dame Lightning."

"Why would he be trying to find a link between the red spores and the Travelers? The red spores were here way before any mention of the Travelers." Karla paused and narrowed her eyes at Sebastian. "Unless he's really trying to find the link between the Travelers and me. I'm right, aren't I?"

"Guilty as charged."

"Sebas, I told you not to worry about me."

"Just kill that talk, Karla, all right? You know that's just something that I can't do so you're going to have to get used to it," Sebastian said, his voice rising.

"Okay," she replied.

"I'm sorry."

Karla touched his cheek with the back of her hand. "I know, baby. You're just showing your concern. But I told you, I'm perfectly fine now. Haven't had a single crazy dream since we got back. Whatever happened to me in the South Pole stayed there. In the past."

"Hopefully, my love."

"Where's Thief now? He hasn't moved in yet."

"He will. Mentioned something about cleaning out his old place."

"Well, I hope he shows for the party. He *is* one of the honored guests."

"He'll show. Besides, Lydia will kill him if he skips out."

"You know how girlfriends can be."

"Yeah, but I don't know if Thief fully comprehends what he's getting himself into. Lydia can be quite the crazy ex-girlfriend."

"Oh, brother. He needs a good woman. Someone to keep him in line."

Sebastian turned to Karla and wrapped his arms around her waist, pulling her tight to his body. "I know I got me one."

"You better."

Just as they began to kiss, a servant brought over Sebastian's tablet. "Sir, this was flashing."

Sebastian took it from him. "Thank you. Looks like I got a message from the government. I rigged it to flash when they contact me."

"Why? Expecting something?"

"Yep." Sebastian opened his email and noticed he had two messages, one from Captain Terringer and the other from Admiral Hankerson.

"You got, two big shots," Lydia said, looking over his shoulder.

"Let's see what the Admiral is talking about first."

XXX　　　CLASSIFIED INFORMATION　　　XXX

Dear Team Infinity,

The United States owes you a debt of gratitude. We are honored to know that the saviors of the planet are good old-fashioned, red-blooded Americans. With that being said, we would like to welcome you all to Washington to officially start our F.R.I.E.N.D.S. Initiative. This will bring together teams of Super-Normals from around the world to unite and protect the planet from an ominous deep-space threat. Yes, we have officially disclosed this information to you. Please enjoy the festivities and then make arrangements to come to Washington immediately.

"Wow, buzz kill. Well, I better get drinking because there won't be much time to party," Karla said.

"All right, let's check the next email, shall we," Sebastian said, quickly clicking on Captain Terringer's. A video played.

Slingblade was standing with his back turned to the screen, talking over his shoulder. "I know you said that you wanted me to join you as soon as I saw fit. But I have to tell you something. You're all in grave danger. Don't trust anyone! I fled from Washington days after we got back after learning the truth. Those aliens that are supposedly coming from deep space—the Rothandians—are already here. They've infiltrated our military, at high levels. I can't tell you my sources on this, but I assure you that the fate of our world is at stake." Slingblade finally turned to face the camera. He held up the knife artifact that they retrieved from Titan. His eyes glowed like Zenith's. "And the time of the reaping, is now."

FADE TO BLACK

ABOUT THE AUTHOR

Braxton A. Cosby is the multi-award winning and bestselling author and screenwriter of YA Sci-fi, Christian fiction and Super-Hero novels. He is also the creator of the highly acclaimed *My Life in Story* Series. When he's is not writing, he spends his time traveling, inspiring, and sharing his testimony of God's faithfulness. Braxton is the CEO of Cosby Media Productions, a media content production company that endeavors to *Entertain the Mind and Inspire the Soul*. He lives in Atlanta, Georgia with his fabulous wife and 4 children.

Follow Braxton @:

Twitter – @BraxtonACosby

Facebook – www.facebook.com/BraxtonCosby

Instagram – braxtonacosby

Website – www.braxtoncosby.com

OTHER OFFERINGS FROM
THE DARK SPORES SERIES
BOOK 1

BOOK 2

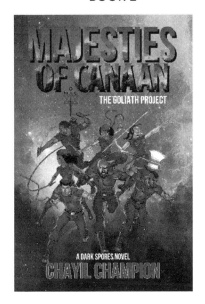

BOOK 3

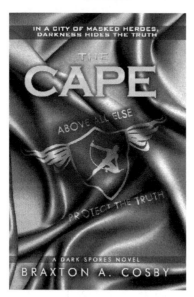

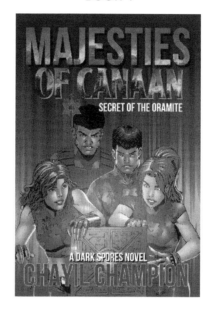

BOOK 4

BOOK 6

BOOK 7

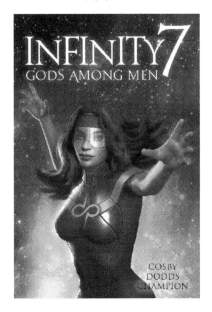

www.cosbymediaproductions.com

Made in the USA
Columbia, SC
25 May 2023

17137476R00109